THE GHOST
TOWN TREASURE

THE GHOST
TOWN TREASURE

BY ANN SHELDON

WANDERER BOOKS
Published by Simon & Schuster, New York

Copyright © 1964 by Stratemeyer Syndicate
First Wanderer edition, 1982
Published by WANDERER BOOKS
A Simon & Schuster Division of
Gulf & Western Corporation
Simon & Schuster Building
1230 Avenue of the Americas
New York, New York 10020

Designed by Becky Tachna
Manufactured in the United States of America
10 9 8 7 6 5 4 3 2 1

LINDA CRAIG is a trademark of Stratemeyer Syndicate

WANDERER and colophon are trademarks of Simon & Schuster

Library of Congress Cataloging in Publication Data

Sheldon, Ann
The ghost town treasure.

(Linda Craig; print 6)
Updated ed. of: Linda Craig and the ghost town
treasure. 1st ed. [1964]
"Wanderer books."
Summary: Linda, her brother, and their two friends
encounter danger and mystery as they search for lost
treasure in the high Sierras.
[1. Buried treasure—Fiction. 2. Mystery and
detective stories. 3. Sierra Nevada Mountains (Calif.
and Nev.)—Fiction. I. Title. II. Series: Sheldon,
Ann. Linda Craig; print 6.
PZ7.S5413Gh   [Fic]   81-16043
   ISBN 0-671-44527-8   AACR2
      ISBN 0-671-44526-X (pbk.)

Contents

A Warning 1

"It sounds absolutely fascinating, Linda," said her friend Kathy Hamilton, "but what a responsible job it would be for us!"

"I know it's a challenge," replied Linda Craig, slender and tall for her sixteen years. Her dark eyes sparkled. "Let's accept the invitation!"

The two girls were seated on the patio of the house at Rancho del Sol with Linda's brother Bob, and Larry Spencer, both eighteen. The Craigs had summoned their friends to discuss a proposal from the owners of Saddle Creek Camp in the Sierra Mountains outside Kernville, California. The camp's four junior riding instructors had left suddenly.

"They want us to fill in for two weeks until the first period is over and the new instructors arrive," Linda explained.

Tall, sun-bronzed Larry spoke up. "What's the matter with the place that the instructors left so suddenly?" As Linda shrugged, he added with a wink, "I smell mystery!"

"Good!" Linda said with a laugh. "If I needed any urging, that did it."

Her brother, sandy-haired and brown-eyed, said, "You haven't heard the half of it. We'll be responsible for some of the trail rides as well as ring instruction. There are sixty campers altogether. Each of us will be in a tent with five children and another counselor."

"Oh, this is a coed camp?" Kathy remarked, chuckling. Suddenly the honey-blonde with an apricot-tinted complexion stood up and announced that she was going to have the best behaved kids in the camp. They would be outstanding in all activities and the top winners.

Her friends disagreed with her statements and Bob said, "I'll challenge your girl campers to a blueberry pie-eating contest any time! Winner to be the one with the most blueberries on his face!"

Linda interrupted to say that they must let the owners, Mr. and Mrs. Rogers, know if they were coming. She and Bob had already received permission from their grandparents, Mr. and Mrs. Thomas Mallory, with whom they had lived since the deaths of their mother and father a few months before. From childhood, Linda and Bob had affectionately called their grandmother Doña because of her Spanish ancestry. And Grandfather Mallory was Bronco!

One by one, the rest of the foursome decided to take up the Rogerses' offer, but Kathy asked a little fearfully, "Are we to be in charge alone?"

"Oh, no," Linda replied. "There is a riding master. His name is Fred Newcombe, Jr. The owners depend on him, because they don't know a thing about horses. Doña and Bronco have been friends with the Rogerses for several years. They live in Los Angeles in the winter."

Kathy and Larry said they would phone their parents at once and went inside the house to telephone. Soon Kathy came back with an affirmative answer and a few minutes later Larry appeared with a grin on his face.

"Counselor-riding instructor Spencer is all ready to take up his duties!"

He had just finished speaking when the young people heard a whinny from the corral. Looking in that direction, they saw Chica d'Oro, Linda's beautiful palomino filly, come from the stable. She trotted gracefully across the enclosure, sniffed at the gate, and then raised the latch with her lips. Putting her nose against the gate, she opened it far enough to get out and walk proudly up to Linda.

"You never told us!" said Kathy accusingly. "Linda, when did you teach Chica that trick?"

Linda laughed. "Oh, I've been working on it for a week. Today she has it perfect. Besides," she added, "this trick is useful. From now on, Chica can open the gates and I won't have to dismount!"

Larry shook his head admiringly. "You're always one step ahead of us, Linda Craig. Okay, you can lead the trail rides and open any gates we may come upon. Kathy can follow you, I'll come next, and Bob can close the gates!"

Suddenly, Bob stood up and pointed. "Too bad you didn't teach Chica to close our gate!" he exclaimed, and started running.

Several horses, finding the gate open, had galloped through it and were now running helter-skelter over the adjoining meadows of Rancho del Sol.

Larry took off after Bob. Not far from the stable, he met Cactus Mac, the foreman, and quickly explained what had happened. The wiry, bandy-legged man could run surprisingly fast and soon caught up to Bob. Linda and Kathy had hurried to the corral gate and put Chica d'Oro inside.

"You stay," Linda told her, knowing that the frolicking horses in the meadow would be more likely to return if they realized one of their number was already there.

Cactus Mac was shouting at the top of his voice and waving his sombrero. Bob and Larry had spread out to round up the horses from the far corners of the meadow. Shouts of "Get along there, critters!" and "Get back where you belong!" filled the air. After a twenty-minute chase, the horses began to gallop toward the corral one by one.

Kathy stood guard to keep the horses from running up the lane to the highway. Linda stayed at the gate, coaxing and cajoling the frisky animals. She closed and opened the gate several times before all the animals were behind the fence again.

Kathy, exhausted, sat on the ground and leaned against the fence. "I'm glad that's over! I suppose half a trick is better than none," she remarked, "but when are you going to teach Chica to close what she opens?"

Linda's eyes flashed. "I'll do it right now!"

After saddling the palomino, she mounted and brought her around to the outside of the gate. Chica d'Oro opened it easily.

"Now, baby, we're going to close it," said Linda, stroking the filly's neck affectionately. She gave her a piece of carrot from her pocket, then said, "All set!"

Linda kept urging Chica forward until the gate was closed, but with the latch not yet in place. Linda pulled down on one rein until

Chica's lips were even with the latch.

"Now push it," she commanded.

The palomino did not understand. Linda dismounted and fastened the latch. She swung into the saddle again and commanded, "Chica, open the gate!"

Quickly, the palomino did as directed. "Now close it!" she said.

The filly hesitated, apparently still not understanding. Once more Linda dismounted, closed the latch, then opened it again.

"Baby, please!" she begged.

Before she had a chance to mount, Chica d'Oro pushed the gate, nosed the latch up and let it drop into place. Linda was so excited that she hugged her and cried out to Bob, Larry, and Cactus Mac, who had been watching, "Did you see that?"

Cactus Mac's face wore a broad grin. "I sure did. I've been tellin' you right along that thar's one o' the smartest hosses ever born. Betcha thar ain't a trick she couldn't learn." The foreman's face suddenly took on a look of eagerness. "Bob here's been tellin' me you're goin' up to the place whar I was born—only now it's under water!"

Cactus Mac said that if they all had time he would like to tell them a story. "Thar's a buried treasure in the hills. Mebbe you can find it!"

"It sounds exciting. Let's go up to the patio and hear about it," said Linda. "I'll stable Chica and meet you in a minute."

By the time she reached the patio, her grandparents had joined the group. Doña Mallory was a Spanish-looking woman with a serene, friendly face. Her gray-black hair was piled high on top of her head and she wore some lovely antique topaz jewelry that she had inherited from her mother's side of the family. Linda resembled her grandmother but was more vivacious.

Bronco Mallory, distinguished-looking with his fine features and tall, broad-shouldered physique and shock of iron-gray hair, was also present.

Iced tea and fancy pastries were being served by the Mexican housekeeper Luisa. As each person praised her baking, she smiled broadly and said, *"Gracias."*

"Cactus Mac, how about telling us your story?" said Linda.

"Wal, t' begin, I was born in a place called Kernville Diggin's. It was on a flat right along the Kern River. Some years ago folks decided t' build a dam and make a great big lake thar. Naturally, everybody was told t' move somewhere else. Such goin's on! Most o' the buildings were knocked down and removed, but a few o' the folks took their houses an' their stores with 'em. All that was left of the old Diggin's was mudsill foundations and mebbe a chimney or two. Now it's all at the bottom of the lake. Whar thar once used to be people livin' an' dyin' an' lovin' an' gettin' born, today thar's nothin' but fishes."

Cactus Mac paused, as if to figure out how to tell the next part of his story. Presently, he went on. "Now, I had a great-uncle by the name o' Abner Stowe. He went off an' became a prospector. Folks say he hit it rich. Then, so the story goes, he put all his nuggets o' gold in a leather sack an' started for Kernville Diggin's.

"He walked to a stage route an' finally got on t' one of them thar stagecoaches. It was gettin' near nighttime, so the driver pulled up to an inn an' told the passengers they'd stay thar till mornin'.

"Well, some of the passengers got out an' went inside. Before the others could do the same, a bunch o' bandits came along an' robbed everybody in the stage an' in the hotel, too.

"Now the story goes that my Great-Uncle Abner saw 'em comin' an' managed to skip outside an' bury his treasure. He was sure nobody saw him, but later one o' the bandits found him hidin' behind some chaparral an' knocked him out. The next thing Great-Uncle Abner remembered was not till years later when he woke up

14

in a Sacramento hospital an' found out he'd been sufferin' from loss o' memory for a good long while. He was bad off with some injury, an' all he had a chance to do before he died was to give the name o' my grandfather—who was his brother—an' tell the story I jest been tellin' you."

His listeners had sat spellbound. Finally, Bronco remarked, "That's a real story of the old West. Where was this inn where they stopped?"

Cactus Mac shook his head sadly. "Great-Uncle Abner didn't say, so nobody knows. Half my family believed the story, t' other half didn't. Some of 'em made a search, but without a single name or place to go by, they didn't get far. Nothin' was ever found."

"That's a shame," said Bob. He grinned. "Why, just think, Cactus Mac, you might have been a very rich man by now!"

The corners of the foreman's mouth curled into a broad smile. "Mebbe I still will be—if you all can find that sack o' gold for me while you're up near Kernville Diggin's."

"You can bet we'll try," said Larry. "I suppose many miners buried nuggets, planning to come back for them. But they were killed by wild animals or died of illness because they were unable to get to a doctor."

"That's sure 'nough right," Cactus Mac agreed. He arose. "I wish you young'uns luck," he said. Then, turning to Mrs. Mallory, he added, "Now, if you'll excuse me, ma'am, I got lots o' work t' do." He picked up his hat from the stone floor of the patio and walked off.

Suddenly, Kathy giggled. "Now we have two mysteries to solve—first to learn what happened at Saddle Creek Camp to make all the junior riding instructors leave at once, and then to find old Abner Stowe's treasure."

"Sounds like a full two weeks to me," said Larry. "When do we start?"

"Tomorrow morning," Linda replied. "Can everybody make it?"

Bronco, looking toward Bob, said in a pseudo-serious tone, "I guess the post hole diggin's can wait for the Kernville Diggin's."

The others laughed. Bob Craig was spending his summer vacation from college digging post holes and erecting new fences on the ranch.

Linda was about to comment on Bronco's remark when she heard the telephone ring. Being nearest the door, she offered to answer the call. She hurried inside the cool, roomy hall with its lovely old Spanish furniture and picked up the telephone.

"Hello?"

"Is this Linda Craig?" asked a girl's voice.

"Yes."

"Are you the one who is going with your friends to Saddle Creek Camp?"

"Yes."

There was a pause. Then the speaker said, "Please forgive me for not telling you my name. I'm a friend of one of the junior riding instructors who has just left. I thought I should warn you not to go to the camp."

"But why?" Linda asked, startled.

"Because of Fred Newcombe," the girl said. "Your group mustn't work for him. He's—he's poison!"

The speaker hung up.

The Missing Stallion   2

For a few moments, Linda sat at the telephone, reflecting on the strange call she had just received. Why had the warning been given to her?

Linda returned to the patio and told her story. At once, Doña Mallory's face clouded. "I do not like this," she said. "You young people must not take any risks. Perhaps it would be best if you did not go to Saddle Creek Camp."

Kathy, Bob, and Larry, stunned, did not speak up at once, but Bronco Mallory did. "Rosalinda," he said, calling his wife by her full first name, which was also Linda's, "I have great confidence in these young folks. I believe they know how to take care of themselves—and their horses, too."

Doña Mallory sighed. "You are right, of course. We should not let an anonymous telephone call upset us. For a moment, I forgot that I never put any faith in them. However, it *is* strange that the four junior riding instructors should have left at the same time."

"I grant you that," said Bronco. He chuckled. "But I'd like to bet my last cow pony that Linda and Bob and Kathy and Larry will solve the mystery!"

By this time, Doña Mallory had caught his enthusiasm. "I believe so, too, and they may even bring back Cactus Mac's sack of gold!"

As the group continued to eat Luisa's delicious Mexican pastries, Bronco said, "If my memory serves me right, it was just a year ago today that King disappeared."

"A king disappeared!" Kathy repeated.

Bronco's eyes twinkled. "King is the name of a beautiful palomino stallion. He belonged to a friend of mine, Mr. Martin, who had gone up into Kern County on a vacation with the horse. It has never been determined whether King ran away from him or was stolen. The authorities have not yet found a trace of the horse."

"How dreadful!" Linda exclaimed. "If he was stolen, I hope he has been treated well."

Doña Mallory said, "We have some lovely pictures of King that Mr. Martin sent to us. Would you like to see them?"

"Oh, yes."

Bronco went into the ranch house and presently returned with several snapshots of the fine-looking palomino. Its color was deep gold and it had white stockings and blaze.

"Mr. Martin told me," Bronco went on, "that King had an amusing characteristic. Often, while eating, he would toss his head from side to side."

"He's absolutely gorgeous!" said Linda. "Since the police never found any trace of him, then whoever might have stolen King didn't try to sell him."

Bronco agreed. "Which leads me to believe some dishonest horse breeder took him."

Larry stretched and remarked, "We already have two mysteries to solve. We may as well add a third. We'll keep our eyes and ears open for any clues to King."

Bronco said, "I know Mr. Martin will be very grateful if you do that."

Larry turned to Kathy. "I think we'd better go home and get ready for our trip if we're going to start tomorrow morning."

"You're right. Bronco, may we borrow one of your horse trailers for Patches?" Kathy asked. Patches was her paint horse.

Larry did not own a horse and always used one of the Rancho del Sol string, usually Gypsy. Bronco agreed to the suggestion and the empty trailer was attached to Larry's car, which already had special brakes and attachments for this purpose from use on previous trips.

Larry waved and set off with Kathy, whom he would leave at her home on the main highway. Kathy's father was a lapidary and ran a shop where he sold native rocks and minerals. He prided himself on having the finest collection of California semiprecious stones outside of museums.

Kathy and Larry returned to Rancho del Sol early the next morning. Gypsy was put into the van beside Patches. Chica d'Oro and Rocket, Bob's bay quarter horse, were driven up the ramp into the other trailer that was attached to Bob's car. Kathy would accompany him, while Larry and Linda would ride together.

Bronco, Doña, Luisa, and Cactus Mac stood outside to give the travelers a rousing sendoff and wish them luck and fun.

"Thanks!" the young people called as they started off with Bob leading the way.

The boys drove directly to Highway 6 and followed it north for many miles. Linda took in deep breaths of the sweet-smelling desert with its patches of Joshua trees and a lone cactus now and then.

At Freeman, the travelers turned northwest onto 178, which climbed up to Walker Pass over the Sierras. Here the growth was quite different.

The soft brown of the mountainsides was dotted with pines and dark green brush. On the slopes near the road, Linda could see wild flowers, including Indian paintbrush and the perky red blossoms of tall scarlet buglers.

"Isn't this lovely?" Linda asked as they rode through the break between the peaks.

"It is now," Larry replied, "but I read some firsthand accounts of the pioneers who came over this pass. Many people perished, horses died, and covered wagons were burned in Indian raids. But nature had a lot to do with it, too. There are deep snows here in the wintertime and whole expeditions were lost in blizzards."

Linda gave an involuntary shudder. "Doña has often said that we don't give enough credit to the early settlers who founded our state."

"They sure didn't cross this pass as easily as we are," Larry said, driving the car down the smooth, wide mountain road.

When they reached the valley, he said, "Let's talk about lunch. Don't Bob and Kathy ever get hungry?"

He honked his horn and the car ahead came to a halt. Linda jumped out and ran forward. "How about sampling that picnic lunch Luisa packed for us?" she asked.

Bob grinned. "Best idea I've heard since leaving the ranch."

Kathy made a face. "What do you mean? I've been filling you with ideas all morning on how we could solve the mystery."

"My error," he apologized with a grin.

Linda found an attractive picnic spot in the bed of a dry creek near the road. Here, in the cool shade of willows, the picnic box was opened. "Mmm, chicken sandwiches!" Kathy exclaimed.

Bob thought that they should not pause too long for lunch, so the foursome ate without much conversation, then pushed on. Their route through a wide valley was flanked by giant mountains, some of them rising over seven thousand feet.

"Isn't this thrilling!" Linda cried out. "And doesn't it make you feel small?"

Larry grinned. "Oh, I don't know. That majestic old mountain couldn't drive a car."

Linda laughed.

After a while, the road turned southwest. They passed through the town of Onyx and finally came to Weldon. Bob pulled into a service station to refuel the car. As Linda and Larry followed, she noticed a horse van attached to an automobile. An attendant was filling the tank with gasoline. Always interested in horses,

Linda wondered if she might take a peek inside the van. She stepped from Larry's car and walked over to it.

The horse in there is certainly restless, Linda told herself as she heard pawing and kicking.

Curiosity overcame her and she climbed up onto the wheel to look through the barred window.

Two palomino colts! she thought. And aren't they darling?

Linda began to speak to them through the window. "Don't be scared, little ones. You're all right. There, that's the baby."

Both colts had stopped their pawing and kicking and were looking up into her face. She smiled at them. "Oh, I wish I could get in there and hug you!" she said.

Her conversation was interrupted by a harsh command. "Get down from there!" a man's voice ordered.

Linda jumped to the ground and looked at the speaker and his companion. The two resembled each other. They were short, muscular, had dark hair and small brown eyes. One wore a sombrero, and the other had on a gray Tyrolean hat with a red feather stuck in the hatband.

At once, the man wearing the sombrero jumped into the driver's seat of the car. The other took off his hat, fanned himself a moment with it, and laid the hat on the rear fender.

"Hurry up! What's the matter with you, Rink?" the driver growled. "Pay for the gas and make it snappy!"

His companion, who acted as if he was used to taking orders without question, hurriedly went up to the attendant and asked how much the bill was. He pulled the proper amount from a wallet, then hastened around to the other side of the car and jumped in. Like a shot, it was off.

"Your hat!" cried Linda, as she saw it fall from the fender. "And don't go so fast! Those poor colts will be bruised and sore!"

The driver apparently did not hear her, because not only did he not stop for his friend to retrieve the Tyrolean hat, but he put on speed and zipped along the road at a reckless rate.

The attendant smiled wryly. "Nice people!" he said.

"Do you know those men?" Linda asked. The answer was no.

"What will you do with the hat if the owner doesn't come back for it?" she went on.

"Well," said the attendant, "I'll keep it here a couple of days. If that guy doesn't show up, I'll send the hat over to our local swap-a-gift fair. This year, it'll be held here."

"What in the world is a swap-a-gift fair?" Kathy spoke up. She had come over to Linda.

The attendant explained that various people in the community brought articles of all sorts to be sold. The men and women were requested, however, to purchase something as well. The profits would be sent to some charity.

Kathy giggled. "I have lots of things I'd like to exchange for something better."

"But it will cost you money," the pleasant attendant said with a grin.

All this time, he had been filling the tanks of the two automobiles. Bob paid him and the four young travelers and their horses went on. Within minutes, they came in sight of Lake Isabella, with its long, bare shorelines, dotted here and there with campsites. The brown mountains rose in a vast ring around the blue waters of the huge lake.

It looks barren, Linda thought, but beautiful.

At the town of Isabella, Bob turned right and headed due north, on past the narrower inlet of the lake.

Larry slowed the car as he and Linda looked down at the water. "So that's where Cactus Mac was born—at the bottom of that good fishing spot."

Linda's eyes danced as she retorted, "Mac has never acted like a fish out of water."

"Ouch!" Larry cried and gave the car more power.

Finally, the foursome reached Kernville and drove along the main street. The shops stood about a public square. Many of them retained the appearance of the old mining days of the area.

Bob went into a souvenir store to ask for directions to Saddle Creek Camp. He was told to keep going north until he came to Saddle Creek. The road running alongside it led directly to the camp.

The Kern River, on the right of the four travelers, was a swift-flowing stream, which tumbled and churned in places over small boulders. At other places, it was free of rocks and had sandy shores. But everywhere the water rushed along with great rapidity.

"You'd never dare cross this steam on horseback," Larry remarked.

Presently, they reached a narrow stream on their left. It was being diverted into a conduit under the road. Bob went past it. Linda, feeling sure this was Saddle Creek, asked Larry to stop and signal Bob with his horn. There was no sign, but Linda found a battered, almost obliterated wooden plaque lying among some leaves.

"This is it!" she told the others and got back into Larry's car.

He turned into the narrow dirt road, well shaded with fir and oak trees. Bob followed.

The road proved to be a winding one and

both boys drove with extreme caution. They came to a section where the creek ran far below the road, at the foot of a steep embankment.

"Nice place to tumble down," Larry remarked, looking past Linda at the sheer drop off to their right. "I'd hate to meet another car at this—"

Larry sat up with a jolt. A delivery truck had just rounded a curve not far ahead and was bearing down on them at breakneck speed!

The driver did not stop or pull over. Larry slowed down as quickly as he could, without upsetting Gypsy and Patches, then crowded to the edge of the road, dangerously close to the steep embankment. In another second, the truck whizzed by with not more than half an inch between the two vehicles.

The fellow at the wheel, whose face wore an insolent look, yelled, "Whyn't you pull over?" His passenger smirked.

Linda realized that a horrible accident had been avoided. She said shakily, "That man had a nerve telling *you* what to do! He ought to be arrested!"

Larry took a long breath. "I agree. But I couldn't prove a thing. If I ever see those two men again, though, they're going to hear from me! Did you see what they looked like?"

"Yes. I think I'd recognize the driver. And the other man had the kind of a smile I just hate—as if he owned the place and didn't care what happened to anybody else."

Suddenly, Linda thought of Bob and Kathy and the horses in their van. After Larry had pulled back into the middle of the road, she stepped out and walked back. To her relief, she saw that Bob had found a turnout and had pulled into it.

Thank goodness! Linda thought, as she returned to her car and Larry drove on.

About half a mile farther along, they saw a rustic sign arched over the entrance to Saddle Creek Camp. They drove in, looking for the office. When they came to it, Larry went inside but reported that no one was there.

"Listen!" said Linda. "I hear people's voices and the rattle of dishes. I guess everyone is at supper. Why don't we just find the stables ourselves and let our poor horses out for a little exercise."

The others liked this idea, so they went on until they came to the stables. These were very new-looking and well furnished. Linda thought, this is a nice home for Chica, and I'm sure I'll enjoy working here.

There were two long rows of separate stalls. Four at the end were vacant and Linda assumed that these were for the Old Sol horses and Patches.

She hurried back outside, where Bob and

Larry were letting down the ramps of the trailers. Linda walked up inside, gave Chica an affectionate pat, and untied her. Then she led her down into the yard and began to walk her in a large circle.

As she came opposite the path that evidently led up to the cabins, she saw a girl of about fourteen coming toward her. As the camper approached, Linda smiled at her, but the smile was not returned. "Are you Linda Craig?" she demanded officiously.

"Yes, I am. We've just arrived. I'll introduce you to my brother and friends."

"You needn't bother," the girl said, tossing her head upward. "I've been sent to tell you that you're not needed here. Mr. Newcombe has arranged for other instructors, so you may as well leave at once!"

Trouble in Camp 3

Linda stood perfectly still, too shocked to reply to the girl. Kathy, Bob, and Larry had heard her astounding announcement and now rushed over.

In a moment, Linda found her voice. "Who gave you the authority to tell us that we should leave?"

The girl answered haughtily, "I am Janny Walter. Our riding master, Fred Newcombe, Jr., is very capable and I'm the best horsewoman in camp. Between us we can manage the riders until the new instructors come."

Linda looked calm but she was angry. "You mean you took it upon yourself to tell us this without consulting anyone?"

Janny stood like a statue, her feet apart and her lips set.

Bob, holding his temper, said, "I understand

the new instructors will not be here for two weeks."

The unpleasant girl stretched her chin into the air. "Fred has friends. If we need them, they'll come to help out."

By this time, Linda had decided she would pay no more attention to Janny but go straight to Mr. and Mrs. Rogers. The warning message about Newcombe flashed through her mind.

Asking Bob to stable Chica d'Oro, Linda hurried along the path and presently came to the dining hall. Campers were pouring from it and racing down to the beach that followed a large horseshoe cove in Saddle Creek.

"Where will I find Mr. and Mrs. Rogers?" Linda asked one of the girls.

"They're still inside," she answered.

Linda dashed up a short flight of steps and went into the building. The couple was seated in the center of one side of a long table. At Linda's approach, they looked up and smiled.

"You're Linda Craig!" Mrs. Rogers asked.

"Yes, Mrs. Rogers. My brother and I and our friends have just reached camp."

"We're delighted," the woman said graciously. In the meantime, her husband had arisen and shaken hands with the girl. "Welcome to Saddle Creek Camp!" Mr. Rogers said heartily.

"We're very happy to be here, but are you sure you want us to stay?" Linda asked.

The couple looked startled. "Why wouldn't we want you to stay when we invited you to come?" Mrs. Rogers replied. "You all must be hungry. We have finished supper, but there is plenty of food left. Please have the others come at once, and I'll tell the cook."

"Thank you," said Linda. She was on the verge of telling about Janny Walter and asking about the status quo of the camp's riding master, but she decided not to. Apparently, the Rogerses were not aware of any difficulty.

As Linda hurried back to the stables, she caught sight of Janny walking down to the beach with a man in riding clothes. He looked to be about thirty years of age and she guessed he must be Fred Newcombe, Jr.

Janny is probably reporting what she did, Linda supposed.

While the four new junior riding instructors were eating their supper, they discussed in whispers this latest turn of events. Linda thought that Fred was disgruntled because the Rogerses would not engage his friends as temporary instructors. He might have mentioned this to Janny and even won the young camper to his point of view.

"It's a good guess," said Bob.

Kathy had been silent up to this time. Now she said worriedly, "I don't like the situation at all. Maybe the reason the other instructors left so suddenly was because Fred treated them badly, hoping they would leave and he could get his friends to fill the jobs here."

"What puzzles me," said Larry, "is why the Rogerses seem to know nothing about this. If Fred's friends are all right, why wouldn't they let them come?"

At this point in the conversation, Mrs. Rogers reappeared and said that the whole camp was gathering in the lodge. It would be a fine opportunity for the Craigs and their friends to meet the counselors and campers.

The lodge proved to be a large, attractive room with redwood-paneled walls. There was a beamed ceiling, and couches, chairs, and benches lined the walls. Overhead lights were electric candles placed in large, old-fashioned wagon wheels.

At the far end of the room was a stage. Now Mr. Rogers ascended the steps to it and a hush fell over the room.

"Boys and girls," he began, "I understand that this was a very fine day at Saddle Creek Camp. Your counselors have reported the finding of Indian arrowheads and a most unusual-shaped snail shell by our two youngest campers, and the brave capture of a runaway horse by an older boy. As I read the names of the campers who figured in these accomplishments, will you please come forward?"

The lucky recipients received badges with the words FIRST CLASS CAMPER OF SADDLE CREEK CAMP on them. There was wild applause from the other boys and girls, especially for the boy who had stopped the runaway horse.

Mr. Rogers went on, "We are very fortunate in having four very fine riders join our staff. They will accompany you on your trail rides and also give you instruction in the ring."

One by one, Linda and the others were asked to come forward and were introduced. To the chagrin not only of themselves but also of Mr. Rogers, there was almost no applause. The camp owner quickly tried to cover this by telling the boys and girls that Linda owned a fine palomino that had won many trophies and ribbons and could also do some tricks.

"You'd like to see them, wouldn't you?" he asked, smiling.

Here and there a child called out, "Yes," but in the main the campers showed no enthusiasm.

Mr. Rogers, obviously annoyed, said sternly, "That will be all for this evening. You will go to your tents now."

At once, murmurs of protest arose from some of the children about having to go to their tents earlier than usual. Mr. Rogers paid no attention and came down off the platform. He stopped to speak to his wife, who was red with embarrassment over the whole incident. When the couple came up to the new riding instructors, however, they said nothing about what had happened.

"I'll take you girls to your tents," Mrs. Rogers said to Linda and Kathy. "Mr. Rogers will accompany Bob and Larry to theirs."

On the way, Linda learned that the boys' and girls' camps were divided by a ravine, over which there was a bridge. The lodge had been built not far from this deep gully.

Linda's and Kathy's tents were very close. Three counselors came to speak to them and were very pleasant, offering to do anything they could to help. The campers, however, looked solemn as they stood in the doorways of their tents and stared expressionlessly at the newcomers.

When Linda entered her tent, she found four cots lined up on one side, three along the other, and three bureaus across the back. Five campers about ten years old were seated on their cots. A counselor Linda's age came forward and greeted the newcomer.

"I'm Marty Fisher," she said warmly. "Come on in and meet our campers." As she introduced the girls to Linda, Mrs. Rogers went off with Kathy.

Only one of the children had a smile for Linda. Her name was Anna Marie Sloan. Anna had a sweet face and reddish gold hair. She asked if she might help the new counselor unpack.

"That would be a great help," said Linda. "I didn't bring much except riding clothes," she confessed.

As Anna Marie helped Linda lay some shirts in the top drawer of one bureau, the other girls began to undress. They kept whispering among themselves and Linda was sure they were talking about her, but she paid no attention. Finally a blond-haired girl spoke up. "Linda, what would you do if we refuse to go to bed?"

Linda laughed. "I suppose I'd ask what you do intend to do. If it's something exciting, I might go along with you."

Marty threw Linda an encouraging smile.

"But suppose we didn't want you?" the girl persisted. Linda remembered that her name was Susan.

"I guess I'd feel very bad," Linda replied. "But what say we forget the whole thing? Instead, I'll tell you about the time a very unpleasant girl was determined to beat me out in a horse show. She resorted to all kinds of unfair tricks."

"Did she do it?" Anna Marie asked worriedly.

"No," said Linda. "As soon as you are all in bed, I'll tell you the whole story."

She could hardly keep from smiling as the girls rushed through their final preparations and dived under the covers. Linda sat down on her own cot and began to tell her adventures during the period of initiation into the Trail Blazers Club. The young campers listened attentively and at the end they begged for another story.

Linda told a short one, then said, "Now, good night, everybody. Let's get some sleep."

To Linda's amazement, each girl climbed from her cot, came over to her, threw both arms about their new counselor, and kissed her. Susan said, "I'm sorry I was mean to you. You're terrific!"

Linda was so happy that tears came to her eyes. She and Marty tiptoed out of the tent and sat down.

"I'm sorry about the children," Marty said kindly. "I've never seen them act that way before."

"Don't worry about it," Linda replied. "I'm

sure they were just testing out their new counselor!"

"Well, you handled them beautifully," Marty added, getting up. "I'm O.D. tonight, so I have to go patrol the tent line. See you in the morning!"

Linda smiled as Marty hurried off, but soon her thoughts returned to her campers' hostility. Suddenly, an idea came to her. The girl who had called Rancho del Sol anonymously had said, "Fred Newcombe, Jr., is poison!" Had he indeed poisoned the minds of the boys and girls against the Craigs and their friends?

Well, we'll just have to make the best of things, Linda determined.

Exhausted by the day's long trip and its worries, Linda tumbled into bed. She slept soundly and did not awaken until she heard a bugle announcing the start of the day's activities.

On the way to breakfast, Linda met Kathy, who reported an experience similar to Linda's. "Everything's all right now, though," she said. "The other counselor with me is great—and a real help."

"Mine, too," said Linda.

The two girls found Bob and Larry waiting for them at the foot of the dining-hall steps.

"How did it go?" Bob asked.

The girls learned that the two boys had had

the same experiences with their campers. At the moment everyone was friendly, with the exception of a boy in Larry's tent.

"His name is Roscoe and he's a real pain," said Larry. "He's a bully and a practical joker. I found a nice little furry animal in my cot—a skunk! Thank goodness he had been deodorized. I learned he was one of the pets from the camp zoo."

Kathy looked horrified. "What did you do?"

"What I *wanted* to do would make a better story—wait until Roscoe was asleep and put the skunk in *his* cot! Anyway, I found out where the camp zoo is and took the skunk back. Look! There goes Roscoe now." A short, slightly plump boy passed them without speaking.

Linda and the others were told at breakfast that they were to report in one hour to the stables. When they reached them, Fred Newcombe stood at the front door. He was a tall, well-built man with sharp features and brown hair combed straight back and slicked down.

"Follow me and I'll introduce you to the various horses," he said brusquely.

The newcomers trailed after him while he kept up a constant series of commands.

"My orders are to be carried out implicitly and I will not stand for any variation," he stated to the foursome.

Linda and the others exchanged glances. This man was going to be impossible to work with!

He stopped before the stall of a nervous gelding. "This horse is named Spot Check," he said. The riding master turned to Bob. "I want to see how good you are on a horse. You're to take Spot Check out and ride him."

Bob lifted his eyebrows but said nothing. He began to talk to the restless horse soothingly. Finally, he thought it safe enough to go into the stall and lead Spot Check out. He grabbed a saddle and bridle from hooks on the wall and led the horse to the yard. After he had adjusted and buckled the cinch, Bob stroked the horse's neck and continued to talk to him.

Suddenly Fred yelled, "What's the matter with you? Get going!"

Bob quickly mounted, but the man's harsh voice had frightened the animal. Instantly, Spot Check became unmanageable. He sidestepped and backed up when Bob nudged him to go ahead.

Linda stood near the edge of an adjoining woods, watching. Finally, she said, "Fred, surely you don't let any of the children ride Spot Check?"

Fred glared at her. "I do exactly what I please," he replied.

At this moment, a stone came hurtling from among the trees. It hit the horse hard on the rump. Instantly, Spot Check reared, and he and Bob almost went over backward. But Bob leaned forward quickly on the side of the horse's neck and pulled down on the reins. Spot Check came down on all four legs. It was a close call!

The instant the stone had whizzed through the air, Linda had looked into the woods to see who had thrown it. She was just in time to glimpse a boy she thought was Roscoe running off among the trees. Linda called to him, but he did not stop. Annoyed, she hurried after the stone thrower, but being unfamiliar with the woods, she soon lost sight of him and came back to the stables.

Linda was just in time to hear Fred say, "If you think you're such a great rider, Bob Craig, break that horse of rearing!"

Bob's face was red with anger. He was thinking grimly, I'm not going to let this man make a monkey of me! He set his jaw and said aloud, "All right, Fred, I'll do it!"

He quieted Spot Check, dismounted, and returned the horse to his stall.

"Report back here at ten o'clock," Fred ordered. "A trail ride is scheduled for that time."

As Fred stalked off, a short, stocky man

walked in. Linda guessed that he was an ex-cowboy. He smiled, introduced himself as Bill Shane, and said he was the groom. A feeling of relief came over Linda. She felt that this man was kind and a real lover of horses.

"We'll see you in a little while," she said to him, "and thanks for taking care of my palomino this morning."

"Glad to do it. She's a beauty, all right," Bill remarked.

The four young people walked up the path. When they were out of earshot of everyone, Kathy said to Bob, "How are you going to cure Spot Check of rearing?"

Bob grinned. "Cactus Mac told me about a little trick. I'm going to use it. You watch closely." He would not reveal what the secret was.

Linda was walking with Larry and told him of her suspicion that it was Roscoe who had thrown the rock at Spot Check.

"I don't doubt it," said Larry. "If I can't do anything else while I'm at this camp, I hope to make a man out of that brat!"

Linda chuckled. "I wish you luck."

When she reported for duty at the stables at ten o'clock, several of the young campers, including Anna Marie, had gathered. Linda had learned that the ride was to be up a steep mountain of firs and boulders, and she knew it would be a hard climb for the horses.

"You'd better put two blankets on your horses," she advised, "and adjust the extra padding well forward under your saddle. That will prevent friction while you're going up and down hill."

She had hardly finished speaking when Fred strode from the stables. "What do you mean by giving orders to these riders?" he cried out. "*I'll* tell them what to do. One blanket is enough!"

As he spoke, the riding master's eyes had narrowed until they were almost shut. "I have half a mind to keep you out of the ride, Linda Craig. Yes, I'm going to do it, and the same applies to your brother! Linda and Bob Craig, you are excused. I'll talk to you later today."

The Craigs were stunned. Kathy and Larry looked at them sympathetically, but felt that any interference on their part would do no good. Without a word, Linda and Bob turned on their heels and started to walk up the path.

Suddenly, Anna Marie ran up to Linda, quickly took a gold locket from her neck, and dropped it into the pocket of Linda's riding shirt.

"Oh, Linda, I'm sorry you can't go," she said tearfully. "Please carry this. It's a lucky charm that has brought my family good fortune for many years."

Linda had no chance to refuse because Anna Marie turned and raced back inside the stables.

"What do you make of that?" Linda asked her brother. "She really shouldn't have given me such a treasure."

"Don't think about that now, Sis," Bob answered. "Concentrate on Fred Newcombe. How in the world are we going to put up with him for two weeks?"

Linda laid a hand on Bob's arm. "As Doña would say, there is always a bright spot behind the darkness. Why don't you and I go down to Kernville and do some sleuthing for Cactus Mac this morning?"

Bob brightened at once. "Okay." The two hurried to their tents and changed into street clothes. Linda located Mr. and Mrs. Rogers, said Fred Newcombe did not need her and Bob for the morning, and asked permission to go to town. The owners looked surprised but granted the request. Linda and Bob set off in their car.

"Have you any place in mind where you think we might get information about the old inns?" Bob asked.

"Let's try that souvenir shop," his sister suggested, so when they reached it he parked the car in front.

The place fascinated Linda not only because of its interesting display of postcards of the area but also because she learned that this building had been the original post office at Kernville Diggin's and had been moved to this site.

The Craigs bought several cards and Linda asked the pleasant woman who waited on them how they could find out about the old stagecoach routes that had passed through Kernville Diggin's. The storekeeper smiled and motioned toward an elderly man seated in a chair at the rear of the shop.

He had heard the girl's question and now stood up to come forward. He was lean, bronzed from his outdoor life, and had bright blue eyes below shaggy black eyebrows. A miner's cap sat on the back of his white hair. He snatched it off as he walked toward the Craigs.

"Howdy," he said, smiling. "I'm Nugget Norton—leastwise, that's my nickname."

The clerk said, "Nugget is a prospector. He lives up in the hills and knows these parts pretty well."

"We're glad to meet you," said Linda. "Do you still mine?" she asked him.

"Well, yes and no," Nugget replied. "I got a little place by a creek. Once in a while grains or small nuggets wash down and, of course, I don't let 'em get by me!"

Bob asked about the stagecoach routes which had run through Kernville Diggin's.

"Well, there were at least three," Nugget replied. "The one folks used most, I suppose, was the Kernville to Caliente route. That runs south, you know." After a short pause, he added, "I'd be mighty glad to go along with you and point out some of the sights."

Linda and Bob looked at each other and smiled. Bob turned to the elderly man and said, "Fine! Could you go at once?"

"I ain't got a thing to do," the old prospector answered with a grin.

As they walked outside to the car, he pointed toward Lake Isabella. "I guess you been told Kernville Diggin's lies down there under water. That was, of course, one of the main stops for the stages." Nugget shook his head sadly. "I've heard it said that there were plenty of raids at that old hotel. Folks took to hiding their valuables because of them. It's my guess there's plenty of buried gold lying at the bottom of that lake."

Linda's heart sank. Had Cactus Mac's great-uncle hidden his gold there, where no one could reach it now?

Lost Luck 4

Nugget Norton proved to be a very loquacious, though interesting, passenger. He told many stories of the area. But some of them sounded so fantastic that the Craigs wondered whether they were legends, as he suggested, or if the old prospector had dreamed them up. Several times they tried without luck to steer him back to the subject of stagecoach routes.

"I'll tell you about the twelve-foot Indian," he said, looking off into space. "Yup, twelve feet tall! If you don't believe me, just ask some of the Indians who live in these parts. They wouldn't go into that section where he is at night for anything."

"You mean the Indian is around only at nighttime?" Linda asked.

"That's right, miss. There's an Indian burial cave in the area. In the daytime, nobody bothers it, but long ago I guess robbers tried to take the gold and silver and precious stones out of there at night, so this big Indian stationed himself to guard the entrance."

"How long has this been going on?" Bob spoke up.

Nugget turned his head, then blinked. "Never thought of that. By this time, that Indian must be just a spirit. I've never seen him, but like I was telling you, not a soul from the tribe will go near that place at night."

"It's a good story, anyway," Bob conceded. "It's my guess that on moonlit nights some rock casts a shadow that looks like a huge Indian."

"Have it your way," said Nugget with a shrug. "But you wouldn't catch me going down there."

Linda asked the old prospector how soon they would come to one of the former stagecoach stations.

"There's one right up ahead," he answered.

When they reached the town of Isabella, he directed Bob to turn sharp left and follow the southern shore of the lake. Presently, he pointed ahead to a couple of buildings. "Stop here."

Linda remembered passing the place the day before. It was deserted.

"That there is the hotel," said Nugget, as the

three climbed from the car. They walked toward a clapboard building with a front porch extending across its entire length.

"This place still belongs to the descendants of the family that owned and ran it," Nugget told the visitors. Near the hotel was another wooden building. As they walked to the rear of it, they passed a doorway with a pink hollyhock blooming at the stoop. A long-handled frying pan hung on the wall beside it.

Nugget jerked his thumb at the skillet. "That was the dinner bell," he said.

At the rear of the inn was a long, covered arbor, and the Craigs wondered if this had once led to a garden. Now there was nothing but weeds and soil.

"Come with me and I'll show you something I'll bet you never saw before," said Nugget.

Curious, the Craigs followed the old man through the high weeds to a latticework summerhouse nearby. At the open doorway, he pointed inside and said, "There, now—did you ever see the like of that?"

From the floor of the shelter rose a tall, stout pipe with water flowing out over the top of it.

Linda and Bob stepped into the summerhouse. The warm, moist air was filled with a heavy odor.

"This here is a hot sulfur spring," their guide told the Craigs.

Around the big pipe was a square pool, bordered with small, pointed stones and an iron guardrail.

"Is the water hot enough to burn?" Linda asked.

"No. Stick your hand in if you like. In olden times, people came to this hotel and used to take a hot sulfur bath for twenty-five cents," the old prospector informed them with a grin.

Linda got down on her knees and leaned far over the pool. As she started to put her hand into the water, suddenly the good-luck charm Anna Marie had given her slipped from her pocket. Linda made a wild grab for the locket, but missed. It hit the water and quickly sank from sight.

"Oh!" Linda cried.

"What's the matter?" called Nugget, who was standing outside the summerhouse.

She told him, then asked, "How can I get the charm back, and will the sulfur hurt it?"

Nugget shook his head. "Sorry, miss, but that's a very deep pool. There's not a chance of your getting your luck back."

Linda felt bad. What was she going to tell Anna Marie? Ruefully, she said, "Instead of bringing me good luck, that charm has brought me trouble!"

She arose and walked thoughtfully away from the sulfur spring. For a few moments, Linda completely forgot why they had come to this place.

Bob reminded her by saying to Nugget, "I suppose that if someone owns this property, it would be illegal for us to do any digging here without permission."

"I'm afraid so," the old prospector replied. "Why—what's on your mind?"

"We're looking for the spot where we heard that a stagecoach and hotel robbery occurred," Bob explained.

Nugget scratched his head. "Never heard of such a raid here," he said finally. "I guess we'll have to hunt for another place. Tomorrow, maybe?"

"We'll see," Bob answered and the three hurried to the car. When they reached Kernville, Bob dropped off Nugget. "Will you be around town tomorrow?" he asked.

"I reckon so. I come in here more'n a little."

The Craigs returned to camp just before lunch. Linda met the girls in her tent just coming back from their ride. They were very upset. All of them declared they had had a horrible morning.

"Mr. Newcombe is just awful," Anna Marie declared. "He makes us do all sorts of scary things and our horses get spooked. Do you know what? Mine almost ran away with me."

"I'm sorry to hear that," Linda said. "What did you do?"

Anna Marie smiled proudly. "Just what you told us last night the girl in the story did. I held the reins tightly and talked to the horse gently to calm him down."

Linda was thrilled. She hugged Anna Marie and said, "Good for you!"

Suddenly, Susan burst out, "Mr. Newcombe doesn't like you and your brother. Why?"

Linda's face clouded. "I'm sure I don't know. But what makes you think so?"

Susan shifted her gaze uneasily. Finally, she said, "Before you came, Mr. Newcombe talked to us and said some friends of his were going to teach us. Then, the very day you rode in, he told us there had been a change in plans, but not for the better. He said we would all have a lot of trouble because of you and we'd better be very careful about being too friendly with you."

Linda was amazed. Her suspicions about the man were confirmed, but the motive behind Fred Newcombe's hatred of her and her brother was unexplainable.

Trying not to show her feelings, she said, "Perhaps Mr. Newcombe was afraid we would upset his orders. I am sure everything will go along nicely after this." But in her heart Linda doubted her own statement and wondered what the riding master might do next. As they reached their tent, Linda continued, "This was my morning for bad luck all around. Anna Marie, I'm sorry to tell you that the good luck in the charm you gave me didn't work. I lost it."

Anna Marie burst into tears. "My mother will be heartbroken!" she said. "That charm has been in our family for ever so long. Oh, dear, what am I going to do?"

Linda told the story of what had happened and at once Susan said, "It wasn't your fault. You couldn't help it."

"I wish I could agree with you," said Linda. "I should have been more careful of such a valuable object. Anna Marie, I shall hunt and hunt for another charm just like it. If I don't succeed, then I'll ask your mother please to locate a duplicate and I'll pay for it." She put her arm around the girl. "I know that's not the same as giving you back your very own locket, dear, but I'm afraid it's the best I can do."

Anna Marie dried her eyes and smiled a little. "I know you couldn't help it," she said. "Anyhow, I made you take the locket and maybe you didn't even want to."

At this moment, the gong for luncheon sounded and the group filed from the tent. Kathy made a point of sitting next to Linda at the table.

The two friends exchanged stories and Kathy said, "One of my girls told me that Newcombe acts even worse than before we came. What in the world can he have against us?" She sighed. "Is he disgruntled because the Rogerses didn't give his friends the job of helping with the campers? Or maybe he's jealous of your reputation as a rider, Linda."

"I doubt that, Kathy. I believe something sinister is going on and I mean to find out what it is! We may not be involved except that Newcombe considers us to be in his way and is doing everything to get rid of us."

"I hope it isn't anything worse than that," said Kathy.

Presently, Linda noticed that Janny Walter was not in the dining hall and asked the girls about this.

"Oh, that stuck-up thing!" Susan replied. "She went home this morning. Janny was just mad 'cause Mr. Newcombe wouldn't let her be an instructor."

Linda felt relieved. At least she won't be causing us trouble, she thought.

An hour after lunch, the bugle sounded for swimming instruction. Linda and Kathy knew it was not necessary for them to be on the beach during this period, but the two girls decided to wander down and watch. Over in the bend of the horseshoe cove, they saw Larry with his group.

"He seems to be having a little trouble with Roscoe." Kathy giggled. "I wonder if that bully is just being mean or really can't swim well."

The girls walked over and stood on a little wooded hillside above the beach. Larry could not see them.

"Keep your fingers together!" the young counselor called out to the plump boy. "Remember you're not a frog with webbed feet!"

Linda and Kathy laughed softly as Roscoe swam along, opening and closing the fingers of both hands in defiance of what he had been told.

"Keep your ankles together!" Larry yelled at the young swimmer.

Again, Roscoe played the part of a clown and kept his feet as far apart as he could. Finally, he came back to where Larry was standing waist-deep in water and stood up with an impish grin on his face.

"I don't know why I spend extra time with you," said Larry. "Your folks sent you to camp to learn things. Just because you can stay on top of the water doesn't mean you are a good swimmer. Your form is disgraceful. Now try once more and remember what I told you."

But Roscoe refused. He said he had had enough swimming.

"Your lesson time isn't up," Larry told him firmly. "I want you to do a special stunt."

Larry leaned down and picked up a good-sized, rounded rock. He handed it to Roscoe. "I want you to swim out to deep water with this, take it to the bottom with you, and bring it up."

Roscoe glared at his counselor defiantly for a moment, then, with a smirk, took the rock. Linda had a feeling that he would pull some kind of trick and watched him intently.

The boy went out some distance, then dived down. It was not long before his head bobbed to the surface and she was sure he had let the rock drop rather than carry it down. Roscoe started to swim back without it. Reaching Larry, he stood up boldly.

"I couldn't bring that rock back up," he said. "It's too heavy."

"Listen, Roscoe," said Larry, "a rock weighs less under water than it does on top. You go back and get it."

"I won't!" the boy answered.

"That's up to you," said Larry nonchalantly. "But watch out. There's a certain horse here in camp with a story to tell about a boy who throws stones."

A worried look came over the young camper's face. Without a word, he turned around, swam off, and in a short time was back, holding the rock. As he handed it to Larry, he said contritely,

"I won't throw any more rocks, but please don't tell Mr. and Mrs. Rogers what I did."

"That's a promise," said Larry, slapping Roscoe on the back and telling him to go up to the tent and get dressed.

Linda and Kathy hurried away, chuckling over the incident.

"Never a dull moment around here," said Kathy. "I hear that Bob is going to put on his cure-for-a-rearing-horse act in the corral just before supper."

"Oh, really? I hadn't heard," said Linda. "I wonder what the secret cure is."

All the campers and counselors had gathered to watch the exhibition. Mr. and Mrs. Rogers had had to go to town. Some of the children were perched on the top rail of the corral fence while the others looked through the rails. All of them were excited and chattering.

Fred Newcombe, Jr., stood by the corral gate, a supercilious look on his face. In his hand he held a ball.

I wonder what that's for, Linda thought, as she found a place with her young campers.

In a few moments, the boys and girls began to clap and cheer. Bob was riding toward them on Spot Check. The horse stepped along briskly. Everyone knew he was in high spirits and ready to make trouble for his rider.

Linda waved gaily to her brother as he went through the corral gate, forming two fingers into a V-for-victory sign. Bob smiled appreciatively and trotted the horse twice around the ring. Then he took him out in the center.

At this moment, Fred threw the ball directly across the horse's vision. Spot Check was spooked and reared up so that his body was almost perpendicular to the ground!

Everyone watched breathlessly. Could Bob keep him from going over backward? And could he make good his promise to break the horse of rearing?

A Strange Meeting 5

Spot Check dropped his forelegs to the ground but instantly reared again. By this time, Bob had pulled a small, bulging plastic bag from in front of his saddle. The next instant, he broke open the bag on top of the horse's head. Water poured over the nose of the astonished animal. Spot Check dropped down and gave a pitiful whinny.

Bob sat still. The onlookers held their breaths in suspense, but the horse did not rear again!

Linda gave a sigh of pride and relief. "Bob kept his promise," she whispered to Kathy and Larry. "Spot Check's cured!"

Just then, Roscoe called out, "Bob, why did the water do the trick?"

Bob grinned. "It was warm. Spot Check thought the water was blood and that he'd been injured."

"Where'd you learn the trick?" Anna Marie asked him admiringly.

"From our ranch foreman. I've never tried it before, but I'd say this is a cure for rearing."

Spot Check seemed very doleful now. In fact, Linda thought the horse had a worried look.

Larry was beaming. "Nice going, Bob!" he yelled.

He turned to speak to Fred Newcombe. To his disgust, the riding master was walking off without giving Bob one word of praise or congratulation.

The young campers were now clapping and whistling. They insisted that Bob show them how Spot Check would perform. Laughing, Bob obligingly trotted, galloped and cantered his mount around the ring. He tried pulling the horse up short and nudging him into quick getaways. Spot Check obeyed perfectly.

Kathy giggled in satisfaction. She said to Linda, "I'll bet Fred is so mad he could bite a horseshoe in half!"

During the evening, the main topic of conversation was Bob's feat. Anna Marie said to Linda, "Your brother is wonderful!"

"I agree," said Linda, "and the more you see him, the better you'll like him."

At bedtime, Linda's campers again demanded stories from her about horses. This time she told them of her trip to Mexico and how she had admired the skill of the *vaqueros* there at roping bulls. Finally, Linda said, "If we don't put our lights out pretty soon, we'll be getting a demerit!" The five girls giggled and without argument settled down to go to sleep.

The following morning, as the Saddle Creek Campers were coming from breakfast, they noticed an elderly man with a mule standing outside the dining hall. Linda recognized him at once and smiled warmly.

"Boys and girls," she said, raising her voice, "this is Mr. Nugget Norton. He is a prospector who lives up in the hills."

The children, intrigued, rushed forward and began to stroke the mule.

"What's her name?" Anna Marie asked Nugget.

"Betsy. I couldn't get along without her. Betsy and me—we're great pals. She carries me all over these mountains and into town. Why, you know, she even helps me find gold."

"What!" several of the campers cried out. "Tell us about it."

"Well, mules are mighty smart—smarter'n horses, you know. One day Betsy here was getting a drink out of the little creek near my cabin. As she sucked in the water, she got a good-size nugget in her mouth. But did she swallow it?

Not my Betsy. She trotted over to me and laid it in my hand!"

The campers roared with laughter and begged to hear some more about the talented mule. The old prospector apparently liked nothing better than to tell yarns, so he said he would be glad to oblige.

"Mules can take care of theirselves better'n horses can," Nugget said. "They never eat what they shouldn't. That's why they never get sick. And they don't run around like crazy when something strange happens to 'em. Just watch this."

Nugget Norton took a can of pepper from his pocket and to everyone's amazement sprinkled it generously on the back of his mule. She stood mournfully looking around at her audience. Then, as the pepper apparently started to burn her hide, Betsy suddenly sat down on her haunches. The next second she flopped over on the ground and waved her legs violently back and forth as if trying to get rid of the bothersome stuff on her back.

Some of the children giggled, but most of them remained silent, feeling a bit sorry for Betsy. Seeing this, Nugget said, "Don't you all worry. You just keep watching."

Within half a minute, Betsy was on her feet again. At once the mule began to search the ground with her nose and eyes. In a moment, she trotted over to where a twig bearing a cluster of needles had fallen from a fir tree.

The mule, using her teeth, picked the twig up by one end. Then Betsy turned her head so that the needles reached her back. Working them like a brush, she rubbed her itching hide. Finally, apparently gaining relief, she let the twig drop to the ground.

"Pretty neat!" cried Roscoe enthusiastically.

Betsy was not through with her act. Now she came straight toward her master. This time it was Nugget's turn to be teased. The mule lifted her right front hoof and with it suddenly pushed against him. The old prospector was caught off balance and went sprawling on the ground.

Shouts, laughter, and clapping filled the air. Betsy's owner got nimbly to his feet, and the children swarmed around the amusing animal. All of them said they wished that the mule belonged to the camp.

Nugget beamed. "I wouldn't sell Betsy for all the gold in Sacramento's banks," he said firmly. "Even if she did bowl me over." He brushed dust off his clothes and wagged a finger at the mule.

A distant gong sounded—a signal for the campers to return to their tents and make beds.

As they scampered off, Nugget said to the Craigs, who had stayed behind, "I stopped round to tell you I think I got a good clue for you."

"You mean about the stagecoach stations?" Linda asked, her eyes sparkling with interest.

"Yes, I heard about one that just fits what you're looking for—a station where the coach and hotel were robbed at the same time."

"Marvelous!" cried Linda. "Where is this place?"

Nugget smiled. "I'm afraid you couldn't find it yourself. Okay if I take you there?"

"Fine," said Bob. "We could go this afternoon around three."

"All right. I'll meet you both at the souvenir shop."

"It's a date," said Linda, "provided that Mr. and Mrs. Rogers give us permission."

Nugget got astride Betsy and started away. The Craigs hurried back into the dining room and found Mrs. Rogers, who gave her consent to the excursion. Then they hastened to their tents to change into riding clothes, since they were scheduled to go on the trail that morning.

"I hear Fred Newcombe is going to lead us," said Linda, making a wry face. "I hope nothing unpleasant happens this time."

When the four young instructors arrived at

the stables, the riding master was waiting. He regarded them stonily. "I called you here early," he said, "so we can come to an understanding before the campers show up. I'm the trail boss for the ride this morning and I don't want *any* interference from you people. What I say goes. Is that clear?"

The Craigs and their friends stood calmly silent. This seemed to make Fred uneasy— apparently he had been ready for an argument.

"Okay," he said. "Saddle up!"

By the time the children arrived, Chica d'Oro, Rocket, Patches, Gypsy, and their riders were ready. The counselors wondered whether Fred would find fault if they offered to help the campers.

I'm going to watch some of the girls, anyway, Linda determined.

Anna Marie and the others from her tent were present, and Linda noted that the rest of the trail group were the occupants of Bob's, Kathy's, and Larry's tents.

Anna Marie whispered to Linda, "You're a much better rider *and* teacher than Mr. Newcombe. Please tell us what are the right things to do on a trail ride."

Linda was in a quandary. She did not want to rouse Fred's ire by giving advice, but on the other hand she did not want Anna Marie and the rest of the girls to ride badly.

Linda made a decision. "You've probably already been told what I might have to say," she said to her charges, "so be sure to stop me if I duplicate the information."

Anna Marie nodded and Linda went on. "First of all, on a ride like this, the trail boss always gaits his horse to the slowest one in the string."

"We were never told that," said Anna Marie.

Linda continued, "There should always be a horse's length between the mounts."

"We always ride closer." Susan spoke up.

Their counselor, although surprised, did not comment. She said, "When horses are taken up or down a steep grade, they should be given a five-minute rest every half hour."

The eyes of her young campers grew large. They all declared they had never received this instruction.

"Do you check your cinches frequently?" Linda asked them.

"Almost never," Anna Marie replied.

"And on long trail rides, do you always carry a rope for emergencies?" Linda questioned.

When she learned that this was not done, Linda again tried not to show her surprise and disapproval, but she felt both. What kind of riding master could Fred Newcombe be? She asked the girls where he came from and was told his father lived on a big ranch not far away.

Linda thought, Fred should know what he's doing. But *I* wouldn't want him for an instructor. She was grateful that Newcombe evidently had not noticed her discussion with the campers.

When all the riders were mounted, Fred arranged them in line. Behind him would come the five boys from Larry's tent, then Linda, with her group following. Behind them would be Larry, then Kathy's tent, with Kathy following. Back of her would be Bob's group with Bob himself bringing up the rear.

The riders set out on a well-defined trail that led steadily upward on a heavily wooded slope. One side of it was lined with a thick growth of trees and small boulders. On the other, the sparsely covered ground fell away sharply to a creek far below.

Linda felt that Fred was going much too fast, and it became impossible for the slower riders to keep a horse's length apart. He did not stop once to suggest checking the cinches, and no rest periods were called.

Finally, Linda could stand this no longer. She called to him over the heads of the boys in front of her, "Fred, shouldn't we stop and check our cinches?"

"No!" he snapped. "I know what I'm doing and I don't need any advice. When it's time to do that, I'll let you know."

Linda felt very uncomfortable and wondered how much longer she dared let Chica d'Oro go without a rest. She had just about decided that she was going to rein up regardless, when Fred himself did so.

He turned in his saddle. "Pass this word along: I'm going ahead to see if the trail beyond this point is passable. You all wait for me."

Without another word, he urged his horse into a gallop and disappeared around a bend.

What an impossible man! Linda thought, as she called back the instructions and dismounted. At least we can take care of a few items while he's gone!

She and her fellow instructors lost no time. They ordered the young riders to dismount, then checked every horse, as well as the cinches and saddles. The campers, weary from the long, hot climb, flopped to the ground. The animals, too, seemed to appreciate the respite.

"Where do we get any water around here?" called out the boy who had been riding directly in front of Linda. He was freckle-faced Skipper McKinley. Everyone looked around for a stream, but there was no sign of one in the area.

"We should have brought canteens," said Anna Marie, "but nobody told us to."

Linda did not comment on this, but she agreed wholeheartedly. Fred Newcombe should have thought of this! She herself was exceedingly thirsty! Had she known no water would be available, she would have brought her canteen.

Fifteen minutes had already gone by and Fred Newcombe had not returned. After ten more minutes, the campers began to grow restless. They started to play tricks, such as putting pebbles down one another's backs and tossing pine cones.

Something must be done, thought Linda. We'll have complete bedlam in a minute.

She walked to Larry at the rear of the group and said, "Fred should have been back by now." Linda frowned as a sudden worry struck her. "Something may have happened to him! Don't you think we should ride ahead and find out?"

Larry agreed. Kathy and Bob also thought it was the best plan, and the three designated Linda to be temporary trail boss.

"We'll go slowly, in case there *is* trouble," Bob suggested.

Linda went forward and directed the boys and girls to mount. She explained she would act as stand-in for the riding master until he returned.

At this moment, her brother rode up to her with another suggestion. "I'd better go on ahead and see if everything is all right," he said. "Then I can come back and post you."

Linda agreed and Bob galloped off.

Larry took the rear position and the line of riders moved on. Ten minutes later they saw Bob approaching on Rocket, with Fred riding behind him.

When the pair reached the trail group, the riding master said, "We can't go enough farther to make it worthwhile. What little path there is up ahead is very bad. We'll turn back."

As he rode off to head the opposite end of the string, Bob whispered to Linda, "Fred doesn't know it, but I saw him talking to two men on horseback. They were so intent on their conversation that I'm sure it wasn't an accidental meeting."

"What did the men look like?" Linda asked quickly.

"One resembled Rink, the pal of the driver of that horse van carrying the palomino colts," Bob replied. As Linda's eyebrows lifted, he went on, "The other man was the passenger in the truck that tried to crowd you off the road."

Linda frowned, puzzled. "What do you suppose they're up to?" she asked.

"I wish I knew," Bob replied. "One thing I'm sure of—Fred Newcombe should be watched!"

Linda hurried forward to take her place in line. Skipper McKinley reined up to make room for her in front of him. Fred and Larry had exchanged places, so Larry rode to the end of the line and brought up the rear.

The trek down the mountain seemed far more treacherous than the ride up. Soon the group was faced with the narrow stretch with the drop-off to the creek below.

Just when Skipper McKinley reached the spot, his horse went too near the edge. As the silty earth began to cave in, the front knees of his mount buckled. Instantly, horse and rider lost their balance and started to slide down the mountainside!

Not for Sale! 6

As the boy and his horse went sliding down the hillside, Linda instinctively cried out, "Skipper! Jump!"

Skipper McKinley did not hesitate. He rolled off his mount's back. Once clear of the animal, he started tumbling downward.

"Grab something!" Linda yelled.

Skipper reached for a sturdy mesquite bush and grabbed hold. The move jerked him to a stop.

Meanwhile, the boy's horse had continued downward on its rump, pawing madly in the air and trying futilely to regain its feet. Finally, he was brought to a halt by a natural earth barrier. This had been formed by eroded silty ground which had piled up against a group of boulders.

Instantly, the Craigs and Fred Newcombe were off their horses and starting down the precarious incline. Linda and Bob called words of encouragement to Skipper. The youngster, still grasping the bush, was crying.

"You'll be all right," Linda assured him, and Bob said, "You're lucky, fellow! You might have been thrown off onto a rock."

Fred Newcombe took an opposite view of the situation. He was yelling excitedly at both the boy and the horse. "Dumb animal!" he shouted. "As for you, Skipper McKinley, you've ruined a good horse! Now he'll have to be shot!"

At these words, Skipper looked terrified. He glanced at the horse, struggling desperately to get out of the pile of silt under which he was half-buried.

"You'll have to shoot him?" the boy said, sobbing.

Linda spoke up in a ringing voice, "That may not be necessary."

Bob, his face red with anger at the riding master's hasty conclusion, added, "Fred, such talk won't help either Skipper or the horse. We must get them both up the hill."

"Up the hill?" Fred cried out. "I wouldn't go near that horse. He'd kill you!"

Again, Linda did not agree. The horse might well have been injured, but a skilled veterinarian could save him, she felt sure.

While Bob and Fred went to help Skipper, she continued on down the hillside until she came to the trapped animal. Staying away from his flailing feet, Linda brushed the dirt and debris from his head. She stroked his neck gently and said soothingly, "You've had a mean experience, old fellow, but we'll get you out of here. Now just take it easy."

In a few minutes, she could feel the horse's tense muscles relaxing. His kicking became less violent. By this time, Bob and Fred had reached Skipper and taken him to the top of the slope. Outside of a few bruises, the camper was all right.

Bob and the riding master went back down to Linda. Fred took one look at the horse and said, "It's no use. We'll all return to camp, and I'll send someone back to shoot this animal."

Linda's eyes flashed with fire. "I have always understood it was the rule of the trail never to shoot a horse unless it was absolutely necessary. Please wait, Fred," she pleaded.

Newcombe glared at the girl but did not retort. Linda and Bob examined the animal as best they could and were sure that with assistance he could get to his feet. Bob held the reins tightly in front of the horse's head while Linda coaxed and slapped the animal on its hindquarters. Fred stood by, giving no help at all and insisting the whole procedure was insane and useless.

The Craigs paid no attention. Suddenly, the

horse got to his feet. Quickly, Linda checked his legs for broken bones or sprains. There seemed to be nothing wrong with them.

Bob felt the animal's shoulders and ran one hand along the spine. Finally he said, "I'm sure some liniment and rest will fix this animal up in a short time."

Fred Newcombe was livid with anger. He stalked up the hill.

Linda said, "Bob, I suggest we use our ropes to help this poor horse up the mountainside."

"Okay," her brother agreed.

Bob called up to Larry and Kathy to let down the four lariats. Then each held one and Larry requested that two of the boys hold onto the others. The campers looked proud upon being asked to assist in the rescue. The ropes were adjusted underneath and all the way around the unfortunate horse.

"Ready!" Bob shouted. "Pull!"

In a few minutes, the animal was back on the trail. All the campers cheered wildly as Linda and Bob scrambled up after him.

When the applause died down, Roscoe yelled, "Mr. Newcombe, why were you going to shoot the horse?"

The trail boss was furious at the question. Instead of answering, he set his jaw grimly and said, "For that, you young busybody, I'm going to take your riding privileges away for a week!"

At this announcement, not only Roscoe but all the other children looked stunned. The former bully was not ready to give in. He said angrily, "You just try that, Mr. Newcombe! I'm going to tell Mr. and Mrs. Rogers on you!"

Linda thought she saw a momentary expression of fright flit across the riding master's face. In a calmer voice, Fred said, "Never mind. I'll tell them myself."

The ride back to camp was made in almost complete silence. But when the children returned to their tents, excited conversation broke out about Fred Newcombe's planning to shoot Skipper's horse and how Linda and Bob had saved its life.

To escape the chatter and compliments, Linda left the tent before the bugle sounded for lunch. She met Mr. and Mrs. Rogers, who were just entering the dining hall to check the kitchen.

"Oh, Linda," said Mrs. Rogers, "as soon as luncheon is over, will you and your brother and friends come to our cabin? My husband and I would like to talk to you."

"Yes, Mrs. Rogers," Linda replied.

When the four young people met them later, Mr. Rogers said, "I've had a report from Fred Newcombe on the accident this morning. I thought I would like another point of view. Please tell your version. I understand from some of the children that you Craigs rescued the animal in a spectacular way."

Instantly, the foursome was on guard. They thought it best to make light of their part in the episode, but to tell the truth.

"I can't understand Fred's being so hasty in his judgment," Mr. Rogers remarked.

"He became excited," Linda said. "For a few moments, everything looked pretty bad." This explanation seemed to satisfy the camp owners.

Before leaving the cabin, Linda said to the couple, "There are three strange men whom we've seen near the camp property. One is called Rink. He and a pal of his have a horse van. I saw it on our way here. There were a couple of palomino colts inside. We met the other two men in a delivery truck. The driver almost shoved our cars off the road leading into camp."

Mr. Rogers frowned. "I don't know Rink and his pal, but they are probably the ones who came here and tried to sell us a couple of palomino colts. What did the men look like?"

Linda gave a description and Mr. Rogers said, "They're the same fellows, all right. As to the other men—the driver of the delivery truck is Mike Olson. He seems to be very friendly with Fred Newcombe and always stays here a good while to chat with him whenever he delivers food. I don't know who his passenger was."

Bob and his sister exchanged glances. Bob's

suspicion that the meeting of the three men on the mountain was not accidental seemed to be borne out by what they had just learned. The two wondered if the men often had a rendezvous up there and if so, why.

As the young people left the Rogerses' cabin, they saw a horseman ride in. He was a big, red-faced individual. The man reined up before the Craigs. He did not dismount.

"I guess you're Linda Craig," he said, looking at the girl appraisingly. "They told me I'd find you here. Well, I won't waste words. I'm here to buy your palomino."

Linda was so amazed that she took a step backward. "How did you know about my palomino?" she asked.

"Through my son, Fred Newcombe, Jr. I'm prepared to pay a fair price for her. How much do you want?"

Linda set her lips firmly. "Chica d'Oro is not for sale."

Mr. Newcombe's eyes blazed. "You're a stubborn young woman, aren't you?" he said crossly. "I have a hunch you're just trying to hold me up for a high bid."

Bob could keep still no longer. "Mr. Newcombe," he said in an icy tone, "I'm Linda's brother. I would advise you to make no more remarks like that. Chica d'Oro is not for sale and that's final!"

Mr. Newcombe gave a rude laugh. "We'll see about that," he said, turning again to Linda. "I'll tell you what. You keep the horse here and ride her as long as you're at Saddle Creek Camp. But afterward," he added acidly, "Chica d'Oro goes to the 3 C H Ranch!"

The burly man pulled his horse around and rode off at a gallop.

"Of all the nerve!" Kathy burst out. "Who does he think he is, anyhow? The Newcombes are certainly some father-son team!"

Larry spoke up. "Linda, I'm sure you're not going to let this threat worry you. Just the same, I think you'd better keep an extra watch on Chica d'Oro. Would you like me to speak to the groom?"

"It might be a good idea," said Linda, who was still stunned by the ranch owner's ominous words. "I trust Bill."

"I'll go tell him right now," Larry offered. "In fact, I'll be near the stables most of the afternoon. Our riding master has given me a lot of chores to do there."

After reporting to Mr. and Mrs. Rogers, Linda and Bob set off in their car to pick up Nugget Norton in Kernville. He was seated on a bench, with Betsy tied to the porch railing of a nearby shop.

"Which way do we go this time?" Bob asked

him as the old prospector got into the car and shut the door.

"Down around Lake Isabella. We're going to follow the Kernville-Panamint stage route as best we can. It'll be a long drive to the station I want to show you."

After passing the lake, they followed the south fork of the Kern River, which ran on their left. Here the stream was beautiful, as it passed through a valley with cottonwoods in the meadowland. Along the bank, willow trees dipped their graceful branches into the water. Mountains rose in the distance on both sides.

Linda noticed brown-and-white heifers grazing in the lush meadows. When she mentioned them, Nugget said this area was a ranch—one of the largest in the county.

About ten miles ahead, the river suddenly turned north. A branching stream that paralleled the road had the interesting name of Canebrake. The travelers next came to a large acreage of Joshua trees, with brush growing along the road, as well as cacti and a fan-shaped type of grass. Linda and Bob eyed the growth curiously.

"Better stop a minute and I'll tell you what these things are," Nugget offered. "That there is called rabbit brush. Good place for the little fellers to hide in. Over yonder is cholla cactus.

That's what the wood rats use to make nests and seal up their homes if they're in caves or burrows."

"And what's the grass?" Linda asked.

"Squaw tea. Indian women used to make a fine tea out of it. Some folks say it's good for what ails you, but I ain't never had much the matter with me, so I never took up the habit." He laughed at his own joke.

Nugget directed Bob to drive on, but in a little while suddenly told him to stop. The old man pointed to a cleared place on the left side of the road. In it grew a large black walnut tree.

"Here's where she stood," he said.

The Craigs looked puzzled and Linda asked, "Here stood what?"

"The stagecoach station."

"Oh!" Disappointment showed on the faces of the brother and sister.

"All the buildings are gone!" Bob said.

"Long ago."

The Craigs were wondering if this could be the station where old Abner Stowe reputedly buried his sack of gold. If so, how would they know where to dig?

As they thought over the problem, Linda and Bob became aware of eyes staring at them. They glanced out of the car and some distance up the road saw an old Indian standing in the shade of a cottonwood tree. He wore faded jeans and a blue checked shirt. He was watching them intently, but his round face was expressionless.

"Maybe he knows stories of this place and can give us a clue," Linda said hopefully.

"Worth a try," Bob agreed, and added, "I've done some reading about the tribes in this area. Perhaps it'll help."

The three alighted and walked over to the Indian, who did not move. He stood with great dignity and waited for them to speak first.

"How do you do?" said Bob. "Do you belong to the Tubatalabal tribe?"

Hearing this, the Indian nodded gravely, then smiled. "Most people not know that name."

Linda had noticed that the Indian looked only at the two men and addressed himself solely to them. Inwardly, she smiled. "I suppose that's a Tubatalabal custom. Women don't rate!"

Not wanting to annoy him, she let Bob carry on the conversation. This was difficult because the Indian did not always understand him and had trouble making himself understood. Nugget, who seemed familiar with the man's broken English, did a lot of interpreting.

When Bob was sure the Indian felt friendly

toward them, he explained, "We're hunting for a stagecoach station where a miner is said to have buried a sack of gold during a robbery. Can you tell us anything about this?"

The old man thought for several seconds, then said, "Station here. I know where gold hidden. Follow me on foot. I show you, but you must not take anything away!"

The Craigs' pulses leaped with excitement. However, they made no comment. The Indian led the way, with Linda, Bob, and Nugget trailing him.

Cave of Gold 7

As the Indian led Linda and the others across the brush-grown flat, Nugget asked him his name. He told them he was often called Mountain Dove.

"Oh, isn't that wonderful!" Linda smiled. "How did he ever come to be called that?"

"Up around here," said Nugget, "we have something folks in most places don't have— that's doves living way up high on the peaks. I s'pect this Indian's family lived near where the birds are."

Mountain Dove had a pace just short of a run and his endurance was incredible. By the time his followers reached the foot of a steep mountain, they were out of breath and perplexed.

"Where is he taking us?" Linda asked. "Surely old Abner wouldn't have come this far and gone back to be attacked!"

"Can't stop for questions," the old prospector

gasped as the Indian started climbing rapidly. "We'll just have to follow."

"Wow!" Bob exclaimed a few minutes later. "We ought to put Mountain Dove in a walk-athon!"

The others were forced to follow fast for fear of losing their guide. They climbed up among the trees and rocks until they were completely out of sight of the ground area below.

"I think Mountain Dove is taking us on a wild-goose chase," Nugget complained in a low voice.

At this very moment, the Indian brought them out onto a spot that was bare of trees and filled with boulders. He wound his way in and out among the huge rocks until suddenly the four stood in front of a cave.

"My people buried here," said Mountain Dove.

"Do you mean your own family or members of the whole tribe?" Bob asked him.

"Whole tribe. White man come long time ago and bury sack of gold here with my ancestors."

Linda whispered excitedly to Bob, "Mountain Dove wasn't fooling."

The Indian led the way inside the cave. There seemed to be nothing in the place.

"Your ancestors' bodies and the sack of gold are buried here?" Linda queried, gazing around in perplexity.

The Indian did not reply, so Bob repeated the question. This time, the Indian answered. "Great spirit come and take away bodies and gold."

Linda and Bob looked at each other, too disappointed to speak. In their own minds, they felt it more likely that souvenir hunters had removed everything. But, in any case, the buried treasure—whether it was Abner Stowe's or not—was not here.

Finally, Bob addressed the Indian. "Mountain Dove, you said a little while ago that we would not be allowed to remove anything from this cave. What did you mean? There isn't anything here."

The Indian laughed softly. "Always something left behind."

Curiously, Bob began to kick up the earthen floor with the toe of his shoe. A few seconds later, he uncovered three small nuggets of gold.

"You're right, Mountain Dove!" he said, picking up the nuggets.

Linda and the prospector also scraped away the dirt, but could find no more gold.

"Who gets these?" Bob asked, gazing down at the nuggets in the palm of his hand.

At once, Mountain Dove put out his own hand to take them. "These go to my tribe," he said.

As Bob hesitated, Nugget Norton spoke up.

"It's okay. By unwritten law, the Indian burial caves belong to the tribe, so anything in them is theirs."

Bob gave the gold to Mountain Dove and the group left the cave. As they started down the mountainside, Linda said to the Indian, "I would enjoy hearing a story about your tribe."

To her delight, Mountain Dove began to tell the Tubatalabals' version of creation. Nugget interpreted.

"In the beginning," he said, "people were animal people. They existed, but had no place to exist. The wisest of them, Coyote, said they should dive down into the ocean and bring up mud to form an island. He himself went down and brought up mud. Most of it ran through his fingers, but enough remained beneath his nails so that the earth could be formed out of it!"

The Indian's listeners thought this was the most unusual story of creation they had ever heard.

At the car, they thanked Mountain Dove and said good-bye to him. Bob started for Kernville at once. As they came near the town of Weldon, they noticed that the swap-a-gift fair was in full swing. It was being held in a meadow.

"Let's collect Kathy and Larry and come back here," Linda suggested.

"It's too far, Sis," said Bob. "We wouldn't be able to do it before suppertime at camp."

"Then let's go in now," Linda proposed.

Nugget Norton thought this a good idea, but reminded the visitors that in order to be able to purchase anything one must also hand over a gift.

"I have a new lipstick in my pocket that I've never used," Linda said.

"And I have an extra penknife," Bob spoke up.

Nugget Norton grinned. "I ain't got nothing but a little nugget of gold. I guess that'll have to do!"

Bob parked the car and they walked up to a small booth where the chairperson of the swap-a-gift—a buxom, pleasant woman—stood. She smiled at the newcomers, asking if they would like to participate.

"Yes, we would, if our gifts are satisfactory," Linda replied.

She and her companions laid their donations on the counter of the booth. "These are very nice," said the woman. "I will take them. Pick out whatever you like and bring it back to me. I'm collecting the money."

As the Craigs and Nugget wandered along, they noticed that some people had brought along gifts of special value that they were guarding. Linda suddenly spotted a collection of rare rocks.

I'll buy one of these for Kathy's father, she

thought, as Bob walked on ahead of her.

The rockhound, who was presiding over his collection, showed Linda several pieces. There was one in particular which caught her eye. It was a rare pink quartz and in the center of the rock was a "bubble" in the form of a horse's head.

"That's fascinating!" she said, and asked the price.

The amount named was going to take almost all the money she had with her, but Linda felt that the pleasure it would give Mr. Hamilton would be worth the cost.

By this time, Bob and Nugget Norton had gone on. She found her brother talking to an elderly woman who was holding several gold charms in her hand.

"Linda," Bob said, "look at this. Isn't it practically a duplicate of the one Anna Marie gave you to carry?"

Linda examined the charm carefully. "It is!" she cried. "Is this known as a good-luck charm and is it very old?" she asked the woman.

"Yes, that's right."

Linda was afraid she would not be able to afford the price. She took a deep breath and was about to ask when Bob gave her a big grin. "I've already said I'd buy this if it's what you want."

"Oh, you're such a terrific brother!" she cried happily. "Now I'll be able to make up a little to

Anna Marie for losing her locket. Thank you!"

Suddenly, the Craigs heard raucous laughter. Looking around, they recognized the man they knew as Rink. He wore the Tyrolean hat he had dropped at the service station!

He must have just bought it back, thought Linda.

On impulse, she decided to question the man, and hurried toward him. Suddenly, Linda became embarrassed. What was she going to say? Then an idea struck her.

"How are the beautiful palomino colts?" she asked. "Have you sold them?"

Rink did not smile at the girl nor show any particular interest in her query. In fact, Linda thought he looked annoyed. His reply was in the form of a question. "Do you want them?"

Linda took a few seconds before answering, then said, "Not right now, but I might later. Where can I get in touch with you?"

There was a long pause before Rink replied. Finally he said, "Send me a letter addressed Rink, General Delivery, Kernville." Before Linda could question him further, the man stalked off.

Since the girl could think of no valid excuse to go after him, she returned to her brother.

"My, but that man is cagey," she told Bob, and related the conversation.

Her brother laughed, but grew serious in a

moment. "You may not think you proved much, but I'd say you found out definitely that Rink doesn't want you to know where he lives. If everything were on the up and up, he wouldn't have minded telling you."

"Oh, you're such a comfort," said Linda, as the two went off to find Nugget Norton. They were amused when they saw his purchase—a large iron skillet.

"Now I can cook me as much as I want," he said. "Never did have a frying pan big enough to suit me."

When they set off once more toward Kernville, dark clouds were gathering in the sky ahead and there was a queer, yellowish light over the landscape.

"Bad storm coming," remarked the old prospector. As they rode toward it, Linda asked the man where he lived. "We might want to get in touch with you."

Nugget laughed. "That'd be pretty hard unless you come to see me, 'cause I ain't got no tellyphone up to my place. But you're welcome to hike up the mountain and see how a poor old prospector lives."

"I'd like to," said Linda. "How do we get there?"

The old man's eyes twinkled. "There's only one way to find me. When you come from your camp toward Kernville, you go past the Indian chief that's lying in state."

Linda and Bob looked puzzled, but Nugget refused to explain further. "You'll find him, all right. Just beyond the Indian, you'll see a ravine which runs up the side of the mountain. You climb up that. Halfway to the top you go to the left and there's my cabin. Except when I go to town fer supplies, I'm always home."

The conversation was interrupted by a streak of lightning that danced across the dark sky. As a clap of thunder sounded, Nugget said, "Here she comes!"

A minute later, the car was enveloped in a downpour, and water ran inches deep over the road. Bob slowed down, trying to hold the car steady on the slippery surface. Fantastic lightning zigzagged overhead and ear-splitting crashes of thunder followed.

"When we have a storm around here," said Nugget, "we don't fool around."

"I'll say you don't," Linda replied. "I can't say I'm enjoying—"

She broke off as a red ball of fire whizzed down directly in front of them and hit a tree that burst into flames. Bob jammed on his brakes. The car went into a spin and at the same time its occupants blacked out!

The Fleeing Intruder 8

Slowly, Linda regained consciousness, blinked, and opened her eyes. Then she remembered the bolt of lightning striking a tree on the roadside just ahead of their car. With a surge of alarm, she came fully awake and turned to her brother.

"Bob! Are you all right?"

He opened his eyes. "I'm okay," he replied fuzzily. As he sat up, Linda heard Nugget Norton stirring in the rear seat.

"You folks sure are lucky," said a deep voice.

Linda turned to the window and found herself looking up into the eyes of a state trooper. He opened the door and helped her step out. For a moment, Linda was confused. Then she realized that the car was facing opposite to the direction in which they had been traveling. She glanced behind her and saw the charred trunk of the tree. Part of it was still standing, but the rest had split off and was lying across the road.

She gave a little shudder at the thought that the car might have been caught under it.

"How do you feel?" asked the trooper.

"All right, I guess," Linda responded. "I—I'm just kind of numb."

Bob stepped from the other side of the car, but Nugget remained seated. "I'm all right," croaked the old prospector, "but I just want to set tight a minute."

"You were all knocked out by the shock wave from that bolt," the trooper said and turned to Bob. "Quick thinking, young man. No telling what might have happened if you hadn't turned off the ignition."

Linda's brother smiled wanly. "I did? I don't remember doing it."

Nugget spoke up. "I've lived in these here mountains all my life and I never came that close to being snuffed out!" He still looked shaken.

Linda glanced at the road-blocking tree. "How are we going to get home?" she asked.

The trooper said he had a saw in his car. "Suppose we take off a piece of that trunk just wide enough so a car can get through. Then the rest won't be so heavy to lift out of the way."

He did most of the sawing. Bob helped for a few minutes, but felt too weak to continue for long. After the piece finally had been sawed through, everyone helped to move it to the side of the road. The Craigs thanked the trooper for his assistance and climbed back into the car. With a wave, they drove off.

At Kernville, the ground was dry and they learned that the storm had missed the town. Bob pulled up at the souvenir shop, where Betsy had been waiting patiently. Linda asked the old prospector solicitously if he felt well enough to make the journey to his cabin.

"Oh, sure. I don't have to do nothing but sit on Betsy's back. She'll take me right home."

As the Craigs were leaving, they smiled when they saw Nugget talking, with dramatic gestures, to a few of his cronies.

"Bet he's spinning a yarn about the fireball," Bob remarked.

Linda chuckled. "I'll bet Kathy's and Larry's eyes will pop when they hear from us what happened."

They found their two friends at the camp recreation hall. "You're dreadfully late," Kathy remarked. "Did you find the gold?"

"Almost," Bob teased. "Tell you about it later."

Larry said that there was to be a barbecue for everyone at camp that evening. "Each person is supposed to come in a western costume."

"We don't have much time to think up ideas," Kathy added. "We'd better get started."

As Linda walked toward her tent, she came

face to face with Anna Marie. Smiling, she handed the locket to the surprised girl.

"This is just like the other one!" Anna Marie exclaimed. "Oh, thank you, Linda. Thank you millions."

Grinning, camper and counselor walked to their tent together.

"Hi!" Marty called. "Welcome to the confusion! Have you any good ideas for a western costume?"

Linda laughed and tried to concentrate. Finally, her face lighted up. "How about going as lady miners?"

"Oh, that sounds marvelous!" Susan cried. "But how will we do it?"

"You all have shirts and long cotton pajamas. You can use those."

"But what'll we put on our heads?" Anna Marie asked. "Miners wear caps."

Linda reminded the girls that sometimes miners wore felt hats. "Let's see what we have around here that we might make into hats."

Eagerly, the girls went through their trunks. One came up with a small brown pillow and said she could take the stuffings out of it and fashion the felt covering into a miner's hat.

One girl had a sewing kit which, turned upside down with the lid for a peak, made a perfect cap.

As the others were fixing up funny hats,

Linda sat thinking about how they could make their costumes even more humorous. Suddenly, she remembered a detail Nugget had mentioned in one of his rambling tales.

When the girls were ready in their get-ups, Linda laughed. "You all look great. Now, I believe you should carry Chinese lanterns."

The girls looked puzzled. "But we're miners," Susan protested.

Linda chuckled. "These lanterns are special."

"What are they?" Anna Marie asked.

"I'll show you in a minute. Wait here." Linda dashed off.

She went directly to the kitchen and asked the cook if she had seven empty fruit cans. She was directed to the trash area in the rear and helped herself to seven good-sized containers. One end of each had been neatly opened.

Carrying the cans, Linda hurried back into the kitchen. "Have you any extra candles and some cord?" she asked the cook.

"Right over in that cupboard. Help yourself."

"Thanks a lot." Linda chose seven short white candles, a packet of matches, and a ball of heavy twine. She found a large paper bag, put all the articles in it, and hastened back to her tent.

Marty and the campers stared in astonishment as Linda showed them what she had.

"Watch," she said. "This is how old-time miners sometimes made lights to take into the mines."

Linda turned a can on its side and gave it to Susan to hold that way. Then Linda lighted a candle, let it drip into a spot in the center of the inner side and set the end of the candle into the soft puddle of wax. It hardened in a few seconds. Quickly, she tied the twine around the can and made a loop handle. As she held up the finished lantern, there was a chorus of "That's super!" and, "I want to make one!"

"Go ahead, while Marty and I get into our costumes," Linda said. They dressed like their campers, but put on riding hats and flattened the crowns. At the last minute, Linda decided to take her flashlight in case the candle in her lantern burned out.

"All set?" Marty asked. "Let's go!"

Most of the campers and their counselors had already gathered along the shore of the cove. There were all sorts of costumes, including cowboys, Indians, boys with false mustaches, and here and there an old-time western dandy. As Linda's group marched in single file, their lanterns lighted, a great cheer went up.

"Great idea, girls!" Bob called as they went past him and his boys.

"And you're almost as pretty as Nugget Norton!" Larry teased.

Mr. Rogers mounted a willow stump and

called for quiet. When the noisy talk died down, he said, "Some of you have never been to a pit barbecue before, so I'll explain how it's prepared."

Twenty-four hours before, he told them, a long narrow pit had been dug. Wood and stones had been placed in it and set on fire. Beef had been cut into small pieces and carefully wrapped in foil and sacking. When the stones were glowing hot, the meat had been put into the pit and dirt had been shoveled on top. The beef had cooked underground overnight.

"Now we need some strong men to dig it up," Mr. Rogers concluded with a grin. "Who'll volunteer?"

There were shouts of "Me! Me!" and the boy campers waved their hands frantically in the air.

To Roscoe's delight, he was picked. He and two other husky boys followed Bob and Larry importantly to a clearing just beyond the beach. The rest of the campers trooped along behind to watch.

There, beside the barbecue pit, the diggers found shovels. With the two counselors' help, the boys worked until they were red-faced, uncovering the meat. The wrapped chunks were lifted out and carried to a long table that had been set up nearby. As the wrapping was removed, a delicious aroma filled the air. Eagerly, the boys and girls helped themselves, first to the steaming meat, then to a relish. This was made of hot peppers, tomatoes, celery, and onions chopped together.

"And look what's coming next!" cried Susan, as the camp cook and two of her assistants brought out bowls of coleslaw, baked beans, and rolls and butter. Then came huge pitchers of milk and bottles of soda.

"Ooh! I feel stuffed just from looking!" Anna Marie confided as she stood in line to receive her share.

As soon as the barbecue was over, various groups took turns singing. The campers who were dressed as cowboys gave two numbers about lost dogies.

After a while, Mrs. Rogers came over to Linda and said, "I understand from the Mallorys that you and Bob and your friends can do some close-harmony range songs. Won't you sing some of them?"

"We'd be happy to. I'll tell Bob to get his guitar," Linda said.

The foursome sang two serious and two humorous numbers. The campers, laughing and clapping, demanded more, but Bob waved his hands. "We'll have to save the rest for another time," he said. Then he grinned and added, "I'm getting *horse*-er and *horse*-er. I think I'm getting *bronc*-itis!"

"Wow!" said Larry. "We ought to dump you in the creek for that, eh, fellows?"

When the party finally broke up, it had grown dark. Flashlights bobbing, the happy children and counselors hurried off to their tents, still humming and whistling.

Linda was about to follow when Roscoe came up to her. "May I talk to you?" he asked. "I have something to tell you."

Linda left her tent group and walked down to the edge of the water with the boy. "What's on your mind, Roscoe?" she queried.

"You'd better watch your horse," he replied. "I was sick today, so I stayed in my tent. Just as I was waking up from a nap, I heard two men talking outside. One of them said, 'We'll get Chica tonight.'"

Linda gasped and cried, "What did they mean?"

Roscoe said he was not sure. "I was kind of sleepy and slow catching on. And when I thought maybe they meant to steal Chica, I jumped up and looked outside. But the men were gone."

Linda was worried. "Did you recognize their voices?"

"No, I never heard them before."

She searched Roscoe's face. Was this one of his practical jokes? He looked perfectly serious. Roscoe must have guessed her thoughts, for he said earnestly, "You have to believe me, Linda. It's true." He seemed a little hurt. "Aren't you glad I told you?"

"Of course I am, Roscoe," she replied, patting his shoulder. "Thanks a million." The boy hurried off to catch up with his friends.

Linda decided to check on her horse. Using her flashlight, she hastened up the wooded path to the stables. At the very moment she emerged from the trees, Linda heard Chica whinny. The palomino's cry had a plaintive sound, like no other she had ever heard.

Something's wrong! the worried girl thought, and broke into a run. As she sped across the clearing, she wondered where Bill, the groom, was. There was no light in the window of his quarters, which were above the stables.

Just before Linda reached the building, she saw a shadowy figure run out and disappear among the trees.

Who is that? she wondered, but thought in relief, At least he didn't steal Chica!

As she raced through the stable door, Linda ran full tilt into Fred Newcombe, Jr.

"Oh! What?" he cried out, startled. Then, seeing the girl, he rasped, "So it's you! I might have known. Look at that!" he said, pointing to his leg. By the beam of her light, Linda saw an ugly welt on his calf below the edge of his rolled-up levis.

"I'm sorry. How did you get it?"

"From that ornery filly of yours. She has a nasty streak in her!" Then suddenly, Fred added sarcastically, "Or maybe she's just had poor training."

Linda held back an angry retort. Instead, she said, "I saw a man run from here into the woods. I thought he might be an intruder."

Fred grew extremely annoyed. "Must have been the noise I heard, but *I* didn't see anyone."

Linda did not pursue the subject. Instead, she asked, "Where is Bill Shane?"

"He has the evening off. I just came down here to check on the horses before going to bed. They're all right."

"You don't mind if I peek at Chica, do you?" Linda inquired.

"Go ahead, but make it snappy!" the riding master answered. He stalked away.

Linda rushed inside to Chica's stall.

"Baby, baby, what happened?" she said softly. "Did somebody frighten you? And you really didn't kick Fred Newcombe—or did you?"

It occurred to Linda that the filly might well have been retaliating for some cruelty to her. There was only a low overhead light on in the stables, but it was bright enough for the girl to examine the palomino thoroughly. She could find nothing wrong with the horse.

Linda came to a sudden decision. After what Roscoe had told her, she thought it best to guard her horse until the groom's return.

"Chica d'Oro, I'll be right back," Linda said. "I have to find Bob."

She flew up the path from the stables and located her brother down at the waterfront.

"What's the trouble?" he asked in concern, seeing her flushed face. Quickly, Linda explained.

Bob frowned. "If there's any funny business going on, I want to be there," he said. "Let's tell Larry where we'll be. Meet you at the barn in a few minutes." He ran off.

A short time later, Bob joined his sister, and the two sat on a bench outside the stables. They talked for a while, mostly in whispers. After an hour, the Craigs became drowsy.

Oh, I *mustn't* let myself go to sleep now! Linda thought. She got up to walk around and shake off the drowsy feeling.

Suddenly, one of the horses inside the stables began to kick and whinny as if in pain. Instantly, the Craigs rushed in.

"Rocket!" Bob exclaimed.

The horse was lying on the floor of his stall, rolling from side to side. His eyes looked wild.

"Oh, Bob!" Linda cried out in alarm. "Rocket's dreadfully ill!"

Prospector's Clue 9

As the agonized horse continued to roll back and forth in his stall, Bob cried out, "Rocket has colic!"

Linda's heart sank. She knew how severe this could be—even fatal. She and her brother must work fast!

"I'll see if I can find some medicine in the stable office," she offered.

"First, we'd better get Rocket on his feet," said Bob.

His sister paused long enough to help get the horse up. Rocket was reluctant, but too well trained to disobey. Nevertheless, he rolled his eyes wildly, raised his upper lip, and opened his jaws, gasping for breath.

Bob led the animal outside and began to walk him around. In the meantime, Linda had dashed off to the small office at the front of the stables where supplies were kept. She hunted frantically for the colic medicine and finally found it in a cabinet. Together, she and Bob managed to pour it in behind the horse's teeth at one side of his lips. Bob held a hand across Rocket's nostrils, so the horse would be forced to swallow the liquid.

"How about my warming a blanket and putting it around his middle?" Linda suggested.

"It would probably help," her brother replied, as he continued to walk the horse around and around.

Linda remembered having seen a small electric radiator in the office. She raced in and turned it on. Then she brought out a horse blanket and laid it across the radiator. In a few minutes, the blanket was warm.

Linda grabbed it up and rushed back to Bob. They adjusted the blanket over Rocket's back and under his belly, then buckled the straps on the side. Bob started walking the horse again.

Rocket seemed to be getting no better and kept trying to lie down. "Oh, what shall we do?" Linda asked desperately.

"We might try massaging him," Bob replied. "See if there's some liniment in the cabinet."

While Linda was gone, Bill Shane drove in. He was horrified to learn that Rocket had colic. He praised the Craigs for what they had already done and offered to massage the horse himself. Bill hurried inside, took off his coat, and pulled on work overalls.

By this time, Linda had found the liniment, and the groom began the massage. As he worked, the man kept up a nervous flow of chatter. "The feed is perfect," he insisted. "I inspected it myself."

Linda, watching Rocket's reaction all the time, suddenly realized that his heavy breathing had stopped and his eyes looked normal.

"I think he's better!" she exclaimed.

Her statement was confirmed by Bob and Bill.

"Thank goodness!" said Bob, stroking Rocket fondly.

Now that the worry was over, Linda was determined to find out what had caused the colic. She hurried inside the building and went straight to Rocket's stall. Everything seemed to be all right, but on the floor she noticed a pail. In the dim light, she observed that there was a white sediment in the bottom.

Suspicious, Linda carried the bucket outside and showed it to Bill. "What is this stuff?" she asked.

The groom smelled the damp powder and frowned deeply. "I think it's a mild poison. Where did you find this pail?"

When Linda told him, he said, "I didn't leave it in the stall. The bucket was probably filled with water and poison dropped into it. Naturally, Rocket drank both."

The groom looked so genuinely shocked that the Craigs knew he was telling the truth. Linda now told him her reason for having been at the stables. "The man I saw sneaking out may have tried to poison Rocket. But why?"

Bill said angrily, "Where was Fred Newcombe? He told me he'd take care of things here until I got back!"

"He *was* here, until after that man ran away," Linda informed him. "Then he said he was going to bed."

Since Rocket had recovered, Bob put him in his stall, then said to Bill, "This whole incident should be reported. Whoever did this cruel thing must be caught!"

"You're right," said Bill. "First thing in the morning I'll talk to Fred Newcombe."

"Don't you think Mr. and Mrs. Rogers ought to know what happened?" Linda spoke up.

"Oh, sure, but I think Fred should be the one to tell them."

The Craigs felt that in any case the matter was out of their hands. Saying good night to Bill, they walked slowly up the path. At the bridge, they parted and went to their tents.

Linda found it hard to get to sleep. She could not put the evening's upsetting episode from her mind. As she tossed and turned, she wondered if the police should be notified. Also, was there any connection between Newcombe and the intruder who had fled from the stables?

And since Rocket had been attacked, Chica might be next! It was almost dawn before the girl finally fell asleep.

On the way to breakfast that morning, Linda whispered the whole episode, and her suspicions, to Kathy.

The blond girl was shocked. "I don't like the way things are going here," Kathy stated. "There's been trouble ever since we arrived! And we don't have even a tiny lead to what's back of it!"

"You're right," Linda agreed. "I thought we had a clue in the fact that Fred was disgruntled because Mr. and Mrs. Rogers asked us to come here instead of Fred's friends. But I don't think that's sufficient reason for anyone to try poisoning Rocket!"

Kathy, never downcast for long, said cheerfully, "Let's hope that before *this* day is past, we'll get a clue."

By the time breakfast was over, Linda began to feel refreshed and relaxed. Her interest in camp affairs was renewed by an announcement in the dining hall by Mr. Rogers. "We will have a gymkhana," he said. "Our four new junior riding instructors will be in charge. Linda, Bob, Kathy, and Larry, will you please come to my cabin after supper this evening to discuss the matter and make plans?"

The four nodded and Linda said, "A camp gymkhana will be loads of fun!" She had often participated in these games on horseback.

As everyone filed from the hall, she suggested to Bob and the others, "How about our going up to Nugget Norton's cabin? I thought we might take two of the best riders from each of our tents as a special treat. If you approve, I'll go ask Mr. and Mrs. Rogers."

"Sounds swell to me," Bob said, and Larry added, "Neat idea!"

Kathy smiled. "I'd love it."

Linda turned back and went inside the building, where the camp owners were conferring with the kitchen staff. She made her request and permission was granted at once.

"By the way, Linda," said Mr. Rogers, "Fred Newcombe reported what happened to Rocket last night. He says he can't imagine who the intruder was or why anyone would try to poison the horse. He seemed very upset and apologetic, but I've ordered him and Shane to keep better watch just the same. Meanwhile, Linda, if you pick up any clues, please let us know."

Suddenly, Linda remembered Roscoe's story,

and told this to the Rogerses. They expressed great concern. "We'll all have to keep our eyes open," said the camp owner.

As Linda hurried outside to her friends, she could not help feeling that Newcombe knew more than he had revealed about the attack on Rocket. Quickly, she told Kathy and the boys what she had learned. Then the junior instructors hastened to their tents to select the children most qualified to make the trip.

After Linda had explained her plans to Marty, she addressed the five girls. "We're going to have a little vote. Tell me, who are the two best riders in this tent?"

At once, Anna Marie spoke up. "You and Susan."

Linda laughed. "Leave me out of it. Name the campers you think are best."

Anna Marie and Susan picked each other and the remaining three girls voted for both of them.

"Then I guess Anna Marie and Susan are elected to go with me on a jaunt this morning," Linda said. "We'll have to start out soon. It'll be a hard ride, but I think you'll enjoy it. We're going to see Nugget Norton and Betsy at his cabin."

"Oh, what fun!" cried Susan, and Anna Marie hugged her young counselor.

Marty laughed. "The rest of you may go to arts and crafts and build a mule!" she said.

Everyone in the tent hurried through the morning's chores. Within half an hour, the four from Rancho del Sol and their eight riders gathered in front of the stables. To let Rocket rest, Bob had borrowed a camp horse. The boys' group consisted of Skipper and Roscoe, a thin lad named Norty, and Davy, sandy-haired and energetic. The two other girls besides Anna Marie and Susan were the towheaded Moore twins from Kathy's tent.

As the riders swung into their saddles, Fred Newcombe came stalking out, his face livid.

"Linda Craig," he said angrily, "I understand you're the one who thought up this harebrained scheme! I don't approve of it at all and I told Mr. and Mrs. Rogers so. You had no business going over my head! I know what's best for the riders. Listen to me, young lady. If you don't stop trying to run things here, you're going to be sorry!"

Linda did not reply, but she flushed angrily. She thought, Is this a warning? Or is he bluffing?

The ranch girl was inclined to believe that Fred would carry out his threat. But in what way? And against whom? Herself, her brother, her friends, or even Chica d'Oro?

The riding master stomped away, scowling. Linda, although worried, knew that for the time being she must put the matter out of her mind. She had a job to do as an instructor, and the campers were looking forward to the trip. Before starting off, she asked Bill Shane if he knew the location of the Indian lying in state.

The groom laughed. "Yes, I do. When you get near Kernville, follow the road that goes directly west. You'll come to Split Mountain. That's where you'll find the Indian."

Not only Linda but the entire group were extremely curious to see what the Indian looked like. As they rode abreast of the peaks which formed Split Mountain, Anna Marie cried out, "I see him!"

All the riders stopped and gazed up to where she was pointing. The sight was impressive. The jagged peaks formed the perfect outline of an Indian chief in a great feathered headdress, stretched out full length, as if lying in state before his funeral!

"That's amazing!" Linda exclaimed.

After the riders had admired the natural formation a few minutes, they pushed on. Soon they saw a ravine that ran up the side of the mountain. Bob felt sure this was the one which Nugget Norton had said they should follow. They left the road, and crossed a wide, rough flat to the foot of the steep gully. It was broad and deep and no doubt filled with a torrent of melted snow during the spring. Now there was only a tiny stream running down the middle of it.

The riding instructors warned the children to watch the ground and not let the horses step on loose stones or gravel. With Bob leading, the group carefully picked its way upward beside the trickling water.

As they mounted higher, the brush on the slopes grew denser. Finally, they saw a solid wall of chaparral on either side of them. Linda and Bob conferred with Kathy and Larry about what to do.

"Maybe this isn't the right ravine," Kathy suggested.

"It was the first one we came to after leaving the Indian," Larry reminded her.

Bob stopped to check their position. "We're just about halfway up the mountain," he said, "and Nugget told us to turn left when we reached this point."

"But we'll never be able to ride through that chaparral," Kathy protested.

"Neither could Nugget and Betsy," Larry said. "There must be a trail into it."

"I've been watching for the past fifteen minutes," Linda added, "but I haven't seen any."

"If we could cut right up the left slope of the ravine to the top," Bob suggested, "we could probably see his cabin from there and pick up the trail easily."

"It might save time," Larry agreed.

"Come on, then," Bob said. "Let's try to break a path through the thicket. The rest of you wait here."

The two boys dismounted, forced themselves into the tangled growth and began working their way uphill. But the sharp twigs of the head-high chaparral scratched and struck their faces, and the tough branches caught on their clothes. The trail breakers bent low and tried crawling, but after a few feet they turned back.

"Hopeless," Larry said as he and Bob emerged from the thicket.

"Well, what are we going to do?" Kathy sighed.

Neither boy answered. Instead, they began to brush off their necks and wrists vigorously.

"What's the trouble?" Linda asked.

"That chaparral's full of ticks," Bob replied.

"Ugh!" said Kathy, and Linda made a wry face.

Her brother and Larry stepped to the stream and washed their hands and faces. Hoping all the ticks were gone, the boys went back to where Roscoe and Skipper were waiting.

In the meantime, Linda and Kathy had ridden ahead on a short scouting expedition. Now Linda called out excitedly, "Come here, everybody! We've found something!"

Bob and Larry remounted and the boys and girls rode up the bed of the ravine to where she stood. They were amazed when Linda pointed out the opening of a natural tunnel on the left slope. It was partially hidden by low-growing bushes, but these were not close enough to the entrance to keep anyone from entering.

"And look here!" said Susan. She pointed down at a mule's hoofprints. "This must be the way Nugget Norton goes!"

With Bob leading the way and Larry bringing up the rear, the little cavalcade went through the rock tunnel. When they came out into the daylight again, they were confronted by a vast jumble of boulders. Bob soon detected a winding path among them. Again there were mule hoofprints, and the riders eagerly followed them.

"I see a cabin!" cried Skipper presently.

Neatly nestled among trees and boulders was the old prospector's shack. Nugget Norton was seated on a flat stone in front of it. Near him, Betsy was munching some white flowers. Linda guessed that they might be some late-blooming wild lilacs.

Nugget Norton greeted his visitors enthusiastically. "You're the most folks that's ever
been here," he told them. "And you must be
thirsty. How would you like a drink of my gold
water?"

The riders, who by now had dismounted,
looked puzzled. "*Gold* water?" Anna Marie
echoed.

The prospector pointed to the stream
alongside his cabin and explained that it
emptied into the ravine. "From time to time,
grains of gold and even nuggets wash down
here."

He picked up a tin pitcher, filled it with
water, got some cups, and told the thirsty riders
to "drink hearty." When everyone had finished,
the children said they wanted to try finding
some gold in the stream.

Nugget brought out a shallow pan for wash-
ing gold. He showed them how a placer miner
would shake it to separate the gravel and dirt
from the precious metal. The campers took
turns and worked hard, but the only fortunate
one was Roscoe.

"I've struck it rich!" he announced, strutting
around and showing off his few small flakes of
gold.

The others laughed and Linda offered her
congratulations.

In his shack, Nugget had a collection of miners' equipment, including a candle holder and a pick.

"How'd you people like to see an old gold mine?" he asked.

All the riders were eager to visit one, so Nugget led them on foot across the slope for about a quarter of a mile. Here he pointed to a dark rectangular opening in a hillside.

"That there was once a very prosperous mine," he declared. "But the vein ran out and the folks moved on," he explained, leading his visitors into the abandoned tunnel.

"It's not very interesting now," Susan complained, looking around at the bare walls. The only thing inside to indicate it once had been a mine was part of a wooden shoring. On the way back to the prospector's cabin, the children ran ahead of their counselors and the old man.

"You know," Nugget said to Linda, "you never told me who it was that buried the sack of gold you're looking for. Is there any reason for keeping it a secret?"

"I guess not," Linda replied. "His name was Abner Stowe. Did you ever hear of him?"

Suddenly, Nugget grinned. "Well, I know the name. What's more, I got a good clue to where he might've stashed his treasure."

"You have!" cried Linda in astonishment.

"Sure 'nough. You just follow me."

Linda called the campers back. She explained to them that she was trying to solve a little local mystery and Nugget perhaps had a clue for her. She directed them to stay close together and follow him.

The old man led them farther up the hill. When he stopped, Nugget pointed to a pile of rocks about three feet high in the shape of a flattened pyramid.

"Ever see one of these?" he asked the children.

"No."

"That's a miner's monument. When a feller staked a claim, he piled up rocks like this to show that the place belonged to him. Linda, suppose you take a look inside."

Everyone watched intently as the girl from Old Sol hurried toward the monument. What would she find?

Stable Panic   10

Eagerly, Linda dashed forward to the miner's monument. She knelt and looked closely at the pile of stones.

"Reach in," said Nugget. "It's hollow inside."

As the others crowded around curiously, Linda put her hand into an opening between two of the rocks and pulled out a battered tin can with a lid on it.

There's no gold in this, she told herself, noting how light the can was.

She tried to take off the lid, but it was rusted on tightly. Larry took the can and tugged at the top until it flew off. Linda felt inside the can and pulled out a yellowed, rust-stained paper. It had been folded several times and Linda opened the sheet with great care.

"What is it?" Roscoe asked impatiently.

"A mining claim," she replied. "And," Linda added excitedly as she read the owner's name scrawled in old-fashioned penmanship, "it belonged to Abner Stowe!"

Kathy gave a loud gasp. "How thrilling! Linda, don't tell me you've solved the buried-gold mystery!"

Nugget Norton grinned. "You never can tell. Maybe old Abner Stowe ran here with his sack of gold and hid it."

The children began to clamor for information and Bob told the story.

Meanwhile, Linda's mind was flying from idea to idea. Nugget's statement was not improbable. Cactus Mac's great-uncle might have first buried his gold at the inn where he was staying and later removed it. If he was suffering from amnesia, she reasoned, he might not have remembered doing this, but instinctively he could have come back to the place where he had mined his gold, reburied his treasure, and gone off without it.

She was brought out of her deep thinking by Davy's saying, "If there's gold buried here, why don't we dig for it?"

"Yes, let's!" Bob agreed. "That is, if we can find anything to dig with."

Nugget Norton said he could help them out a little. He returned to his cabin and came back with several shovels and picks. The Old Solers got busy with these, while the children dug with sharp, pointed rocks. Within a short time, a large area had been torn up around the miner's monument. Davy had unearthed part of an Indian's ax and Roscoe had found a couple of arrowheads. But there was no sign of any gold, either in a sack or lying loose.

Finally, Bob looked at his wristwatch. "Good night!" he cried. "We'll never make it back to camp in time for lunch, and we didn't bring any food with us."

Nugget's face broke into a broad grin. "If you all don't mind sharing with Betsy and me," he said, "we can fix you up with some bread and ham and canned peaches. For your drink, I can offer more gold water."

The riding instructors looked at one another. They knew they would be at least an hour behind schedule. Fifteen more minutes would not matter. Before they could make up their minds what to do, several of the children called out, "Let's eat with Betsy!"

Linda laughed and at a signal from her companions said, "I guess you win."

Nugget's invitation was accepted and they all returned to his cabin. The riders found places to relax under the trees and made their own sandwiches from thick slices of rye bread and canned ham. At the end of the meal, Anna Marie declared this was the "most fun picnic" she had ever attended.

Before the riders left, Linda and Bob asked Nugget if he would take them to another stage-coach station sometime soon.

"I sure will. How about this afternoon? Me and Betsy have no dates."

The Craigs laughed and said they thought this would be all right. There was to be a long rehearsal for the play that their campers were to give. "We'll meet you at the general store about three o'clock," Linda proposed. "If we're not there by four, don't wait for us."

"Very good," the prospector agreed.

After thanking the old man for his hospitality, the riders mounted up and headed for camp. As they were going along the road beside the river, they reached a point where it was strewn with boulders and the water tumbled along at great speed.

Larry pointed out some leaping fish in the sparkling water. "Too bad we haven't a pole and line. Maybe we could catch them."

Davy seemed fascinated by the sight. "I'll bet I could get one with my bare hands," he boasted.

"I'd like to see you," Roscoe replied with a laugh.

In a flash, Davy jumped from his horse. He threw the reins to Larry and yelled, "I'll show you!"

"Where are you going?" Larry called to him in astonishment.

Davy merely grinned and did not answer. He dashed to the water and began jumping from boulder to boulder toward the leaping fish.

"He's crazy!" Bob cried out, swinging from his saddle and handing the lines to Roscoe.

Anna Marie, looking on fearfully, screamed, "Davy's going to be drowned!"

By this time, the boy was well out into the river. Linda could see that he was in danger of losing his balance on the slippery boulders any moment!

Bob and Larry had reached the bank and were yelling at the boy to come back. Davy paid no attention and leaped to another rock. He slipped, and teetered for a few seconds, with his arms flailing the air. Then he fell into the stream! Davy tried desperately to get to his feet, but the current swept his body along, slamming it against the rocks.

By this time, Bob and Larry were in the water. They knew that the best way to maintain their footing was to hold hands. They did this and made a beeline for Davy. Though finding it difficult to keep from being swept off balance, the two kept on doggedly and finally caught up with Davy. They both grabbed the boy's arms and stood him upright. Now the three gripped hands, and made their way toward shore, keeping close together.

Linda and the others waited breathlessly until Davy and his rescuers were safely on land. The boy hung his head. "I—I didn't know it was so bad!" he said, fighting back tears. "Thanks, Bob and Larry. I guess you saved my life."

The young camper was bruised and shocked from his fright. Larry lifted him onto Gypsy so the boy could ride with him the rest of the way to camp. They led Davy's mount behind them.

When the procession reached Saddle Creek Camp and reined up at the stables, Fred Newcombe was waiting for them, a dour look on his face. The children gave him no chance to find fault. They began at once to tell the riding master what a wonderful adventure they had had.

Susan added, "It's our best ride so far!"

Newcombe showed no pleasure at this report, and although Davy was still wet, he asked no questions. Instead, he glared at the Craigs and their friends, ordered the children to rub down their own horses and to stable them, then stalked away.

Bob sent Davy off to change his clothes and Linda told her campers to go directly to the tent as soon as their work with the horses was finished. She would see them there. After Chica d'Oro was stabled, Linda went to the Rogerses' cabin to explain why they were late.

"We weren't worried," said Mrs. Rogers. "We trust you implicitly with the children and the horses."

Mr. Rogers smiled. "I hope you didn't starve our young campers."

"Oh, no indeed. They ate a miner's lunch," Linda said, smiling back at them. "And now I have another request. Would you mind if Bob and I go out and do a little sleuthing? You see, we're trying to solve a mystery for the foreman at our ranch. He used to live in Kernville Diggin's. At this moment, our chances don't look too good. But at least we might come across another nice ride for the children."

"You go right ahead," said Mr. Rogers, "and I wish you luck in your sleuthing."

"I do, too," Mrs. Rogers added, smiling. "I hate unsolved mysteries."

Linda left and was halfway to her tent when she became aware of a great commotion at the stables. Horses were whinnying and kicking and she could hear Newcombe shouting at the top of his voice.

More trouble! Linda thought. Panic for Chica's safety almost overcame her as she ran toward the stables.

The noise grew louder as she approached. Campers and counselors were running from all directions to see what had happened. Fred Newcombe stood outside the building, ordering everyone to stay back.

When he saw Linda coming, the riding master said, "Here comes one of the people responsible for all this trouble! Everything was calm and peaceful around here until you came back from that ride and put the horses away." He glared at the girl. "I'm not going to stand for it any longer!" Newcombe ranted. "You four are going to leave this camp!"

Linda stopped abruptly, her heart thumping. Could Fred Newcombe carry out his order? The girl determined to stand her ground.

"Whatever is the matter in there," Linda said icily, "I had nothing to do with it. Neither did my brother or Kathy or Larry!"

She tried to enter the stables, but Newcombe would not let her pass. Fortunately, Bob and Larry arrived at this point and the three insisted upon going inside.

"I want to find out what the racket's all about," said Bob. "Maybe we can do something to stop it."

Unable to hold them back, Newcombe stepped aside, giving the trio a look of hatred. The pawing, whinnying, and kicking continued. Linda flew toward Chica.

"Baby, what is it?" she asked fearfully. "What frightened you? Or do you have a pain?"

Linda suddenly realized that Gypsy, Patches, and three of the camp horses were acting the same way. This struck her as strange. Why had certain horses been affected and not others?

She experienced a chill of fear as she wondered if they, too, might have been given poisoned water to drink. There was no bucket in Chica's stall, but Linda looked at the palomino's lips. Was it her imagination or were they swollen?

She dashed over to examine Gypsy. The horse's lips had the same peculiar look! So did those of Patches and the three camp animals.

"Bob!" Linda exclaimed. "Someone has put a stinging acid on these horses' lips!"

Her brother's face was gray. "I'm afraid you're right, Linda."

They went into a huddle with Larry, who said, "I think it's really getting dangerous around here. For the sake of our horses, maybe we'd better pull out."

"And leave the camp stranded?" Linda asked in dismay.

"At least we could suggest to Mr. Rogers that he get substitutes immediately," he argued. "Of course, Gypsy belongs to you, but I'm pretty fond of the old gal. I'd hate to see anything happen to her."

"In the meantime, let's get these poor animals some water and apply salve to their lips," Bob urged.

At this moment, Bill Shane came running in and Fred Newcombe left. Upon seeing the injured horses, he closed his eyes in distress. "These things always happen when I'm away," he said. "We were low on oats, so I took just a little time to run down to Kernville and get some." The groom's shoulders sagged. "Mr. Newcombe is going to blame me, but I want you all to know that I had nothing to do with this."

He helped the young instructors to treat the horses' burning lips and quiet the animals. Finally, order was restored in the stables.

By this time, Mr. and Mrs. Rogers had arrived on the scene. Both were extremely upset and took Larry and the Craigs aside.

Mrs. Rogers said, "If you four will stay all summer, we will dismiss Mr. Newcombe and Bill Shane. There has been too much trouble here and we don't want any more."

"I'm sorry," said Linda, "but it would be impossible for us to stay for another month. Actually, we can't prove that these men are responsible."

"That's true," Mr. Rogers conceded, "but there is one thing I *can* do immediately—get a carpenter up here from Kernville to put bars on all the stable windows and padlocks on the front and back doors. The only persons to have keys will be my wife and I, Fred Newcombe, Bill Shane, and you Craigs."

"Which means," said Bob, "that if anything more goes wrong here, you'll know the culprit. It will be one of the holders of a key."

Mr. Rogers smiled. "I do not mean to imply that I think you young people are dishonest. My idea is that the two men will not feel suspicion is being cast upon them alone. And, of course, it may turn out that someone from the outside is responsible for everything."

After the couple had gone, the young instructors left the stables. Larry had promised to play baseball with some of the boys and went off to the diamond.

Bob paused near the lot where the Craigs' car was parked with several others. He glanced at his watch. "We ought to leave now, Sis, if we expect to meet Nugget at three."

Linda, deep in thought, did not reply at once. Then she said, "I think it might be more important for us to keep an eye on Fred Newcombe, and if he leaves here, to trail him."

"I'm with you," Bob replied.

The two turned back and entered the woods near the stables. Hiding separately, they kept watch on both the stable and the lot. About ten minutes later, Bob saw the riding master hurry down the path, get into his car and drive off. The Craigs jumped into theirs, waited a moment, then followed him.

At the entrance, he turned away from Kernville on the dirt road. Bob was careful to keep out of sight of the car ahead, but trailed it easily by the dust it raised.

Newcombe drove for about a mile, then suddenly turned sharp right onto a narrow dirt lane that led up the mountainside. Soon it became little more than a trail, which wound between heavily wooded hillsides. Gradually, the growth on the slopes grew sparse and boulders took their place. Here and there, a spiny, treelike yucca plant stood tall and straight.

As the road grew narrower and rougher, Bob stopped. "He can't go much farther on this," he said.

Ahead of them, around a bend, they heard a car's motor stop. Apparently, Newcombe was having the same problem.

Swiftly, Bob and Linda alighted. They ran to

the bend and peered around it. Newcombe was already striding up a narrow trail. The Craigs followed.

With Bob some paces ahead of his sister, they followed the man along the rough, twisting trail. It grew steeper and soon they lost sight of him among the huge boulders above them.

Suddenly, Bob's ears caught a slight noise above them, and he glanced up. Hurtling through the air toward his sister was a big yucca plant!

"Look out!" he cried in alarm.

But Linda could not sidestep in time. The sharp, spiny leaves of the yucca struck her full force!

The Special Stagecoach 11

Linda was thrown to the ground by the force of the yucca.

Instantly, Bob sprang to help her. "Linda, are you hurt?" he asked anxiously.

"No." She took a deep breath and stood up. "I'm all right. Lucky I was wearing this big hat, or my face would be a mess."

Linda's neck and hands, however, were covered with scratches. She surveyed the yucca thoughtfully. "I'm glad the plant wasn't any heavier." Then, as she fully collected her wits, Linda added, "This yucca didn't tumble down of its own accord. I'm sure someone threw it at me!"

"I *know* someone did," her brother said. "It was Rink!"

"What!"

Bob told her that in the split-second before

the plant had struck her he had seen a man duck behind a boulder on the slope above. "He wore a Tyrolean hat!"

"I'm not surprised," said Linda.

Together the Craigs examined the plant. At the base just below the collar of spines were marks showing it had been hacked off with a sharp knife. Linda looked up the slope and her eyes flashed with anger. "Let's go find Rink!"

"No!" Bob said firmly. "We're unfamiliar with this territory. Newcombe is probably up there with him right now, watching us. We'd be sitting ducks."

Linda did not argue. She realized the wisdom of her brother's decision. When they reached the car, Bob backed it all the way out the narrow dirt road.

It was not until they were on the road to camp that either of them spoke. Linda said she was disappointed not to have seen where Newcombe was going.

"Every time we almost catch him in something suspicious he disappears or gets out of it."

"Cheer up," counseled Bob. "There's no doubt in my mind that Newcombe was on his way to meet Rink and didn't want us to find out what they're up to."

Linda agreed. "I wonder how Fred will act when we meet again."

Bob said he was sure the man would deny any accusations or acquaintanceship with Rink. "And we still have no proof that he's involved in anything underhanded."

Linda sighed. Then she asked Bob to pull to the side of the road so she could go down to the pretty creek they were passing. "Some ice-cold water on my neck and hands will feel good."

Her brother parked and waited while Linda bathed her scratches. She also washed her face, and shook out her hat to reshape it. When she returned, she declared she felt much better.

"Let's not go back to camp," Linda suggested. "I feel all right—really I do. I'd like to keep our appointment with Nugget Norton."

Bob glanced at his watch. "Okay. We'll be late, but he may still be there."

When they reached the town, the old prospector was seated on the bench where they had found him before and Betsy was tied to the same railing. As the car approached, Nugget got up and called a cheery greeting.

"Climb aboard!" Bob said.

As soon as the old man was in the rear seat and the door closed, he said, "Today we're going in a different direction. One of the old stage routes led from here to Tailholt and northern California in a northwesterly direction.

"But to pick up that route," the old prospector continued, "We've first got to go south to Wofford Heights."

When they reached this town, Nugget directed Bob to turn sharp right. Soon the road was climbing up into Greenhorn Mountain, through which Portuguese Pass ran.

"You know," said Nugget, "back in the old mining days, lots of Chinese and Portuguese came here. They were good workers and after the Americans thought a mine was played out, the immigrants would stay on and clean up the leavings."

At Alta Sierra, the old prospector told Bob to turn right once more. As they drove along the mountain road, they passed Sunday Peak. "Elevation, eight thousand feet," Nugget announced proudly. Here and there he pointed out the old stagecoach route. It was now a rutted, grass-grown strip. After a while, the road they were on grew rocky and rough.

"Better slow down, Bob," Linda advised. "You might break a spring."

Nugget Norton chuckled. "I'll bet you there was many a spring broke on those stages long ago."

"And riding in them must have been frightful," Linda commented, her admiration for the old-time travelers rising.

The road went up and down hill, over deep

ruts, and at times through heavily wooded sections.

"I want you to notice the sugar-pine trees," said Nugget. "The cones hang different from most evergreen trees. See, there's one pair of 'em at the end of each branch."

"And they're enormous!" Linda remarked.

Just then, the car went into a rut and bounced violently. Bob applied the brake.

"This car can't take much more of this," he said.

"That's okay," replied Nugget. "We can walk."

He got out and led them down a steep, tree-shaded gully. At the bottom, they emerged into a sunny meadow.

"This was the old Pattengil place," said the prospector. "A long time ago, there was a building on it that was a stagecoach station. Look around. Maybe you'll find the buried sack of gold!"

Linda gazed over the soft green grass toward the far side of the meadow where a line of willows bordered a stream.

"Not a thing is left," she remarked, disappointed.

"There's an apple orchard," Bob said with a grin.

"And it's close to a hundred years old," the prospector informed them.

The Craigs began exploring. Linda noticed an almost obliterated road running through the meadow, and near it a grass-covered rectangle a little higher than the rest of the ground.

"Maybe the house stood here," Linda said and began searching. In a few minutes, she had found several pieces of broken crockery.

"This was the place, all right," Bob remarked.

"Long ago," said Nugget, "this was an Indian encampment. Funny how a property has a lot of folks on it, then a few, and finally nobody."

The Craigs were trying to reconstruct in their minds what the place had looked like when it was a stagecoach stop. "And," said Linda, "if this was the station Abner Stowe stayed at, where could he have buried the gold?"

As they thought over the question, a jeep came roaring out of the gully road and pulled up nearby. A slender young man alighted and walked up to the group.

"You find any treasures?" he asked pleasantly.

"Yes," Linda replied, smiling, and showed the pieces of pottery.

"I'm a relic hunter, too," the stranger said. "And the old West is my hobby. I know this spot well. If you're interested, maybe I can tell you something about it." He put out his hand. "The name's Elliott."

"We'd love some information," Linda told him. "Did you ever hear of a bandit raid on this place soon after a stagecoach had pulled in?"

Mr. Elliott shook his head. "I never heard of such an incident." He studied the Craigs curiously. "Have you any special reason for wanting to know?"

Linda answered cagily, "A friend of ours had a forebear who was supposed to have buried something at that time, but was never able to retrieve it. We'd love to find it for him."

"Your best bet," said Mr. Elliott, "is to learn on which stagecoach line this raid happened."

Bob grinned. "We've been trying for several days to do just that. But so far we haven't had any luck."

The relic hunter was thoughtful a few seconds; then he asked, "How many horses pulled the stagecoach to which you refer?"

"We don't know," Linda answered. "Were different numbers used?"

"Yes. On the long, hard runs there were four horses. But on one of our local runs—from Isabella to Onyx—only two animals pulled the stage."

Linda was excited to hear this. She made up her mind to find out as soon as she could get to a telephone if Cactus Mac could answer the question. In a few minutes, they said good-bye to Mr. Elliott and walked up the gully to their car and headed for Kernville. As soon as they reached town, Linda thanked Nugget and said good-bye, then went to call Rancho del Sol.

"Doña?" she asked, as a woman answered.

"Yes. Linda? How glad I am to hear from you!"

"We're having a wonderfully exciting time," Linda said and told of their search for the sack of gold.

"Is Cactus Mac around?" she added. "I'd like to find out something from him that may provide a clue."

When the foreman came on the line, Linda asked, "Do you know how many horses pulled the stage on which your great-uncle rode?"

There was a short pause. "Funny you should ask me that," said Cactus Mac. "I sure never would've thought of it. But now I remember plain as day. Only two horses pulled that stage."

Linda could have shouted for joy. The search was narrowing! She told Cactus Mac what sleuthing she and Bob had done so far and he thanked her profusely.

"You been mighty kind," he said. "I didn't mean for you t' go t' such a heap o' trouble."

"Oh, we've been enjoying ourselves," Linda

assured him. "Now we can concentrate on the stage from Isabella to Onyx."

When Linda returned to Bob, her face was one big smile. "I have a real clue this time!" she said, and reported what Cactus had said about the two-horse stage. "Now I have great hopes of solving the mystery soon!"

He warned her not to become too enthusiastic. "Don't forget that someone else may already have dug up that gold long ago."

Linda made a face at her brother. "Remember what Doña always advises: Hold good thoughts and your wishes are more likely to come true than if you don't."

Her brother laughed. "I'll start right now, and wish not only that we locate the treasure, but also that we'll find out the truth about Fred Newcombe's actions."

When they reached Saddle Creek Camp and saw the stables, the Craigs were delighted. Bars had been put across the windows and there were padlocks on both doors.

"I hope," said Bob, "that Fred won't think up another way to blame us if something else happens to the horses."

Linda's eyes flashed. "He'd better not try!"

They talked for a few minutes with Bill Shane and learned from him that the riding master was not expected back that evening. He had gone to his father's ranch to spend the night.

"When did you learn this?" Linda asked quickly.

"He called up about ten minutes ago," Bill replied.

The Craigs looked at each other. There was no doubt in their minds but that Fred Newcombe, Jr., was staying away on purpose. He was not ready yet to face Linda and Bob and be questioned.

The brother and sister hurried off to their tents. Linda's girls were in theirs, getting ready for supper.

"Guess what, Linda!" Anna Marie exclaimed. "This afternoon I heard about a ghost town!"

"A ghost town?" Linda repeated.

"Yes, a real one. Will you take us there sometime soon?"

"That depends, of course, on where it is," her young counselor replied cautiously.

"Oh, it isn't terribly far from here," said Anna Marie. Her eyes grew large. "Besides, you haven't found that buried gold yet. Maybe it's in the ghost town!"

The Danger Gate   *12*

"Where did you hear about this ghost town?"
Linda asked Anna Marie.

Her younger camper said an elderly woman
had driven in from a ranch somewhere on the
other side of Kern River above Lake Isabella.

"And what do you think she had with her?"
Susan broke in. "A baby lamb and a baby
goat!"

"I'll bet they were darling," Linda remarked,
although her thoughts were still on the ghost
town.

Susan explained, "The woman wanted Mr.
and Mrs. Rogers to buy the animals for our
camp zoo. They said they'd think it over. Oh, I
hope they do!"

Anna Marie also was more interested in the
ghost town. "Linda, won't you please take us
there?" she asked.

"It sounds interesting," Linda admitted, and thought, I could combine my job as riding instructor with a little sleuthing.

"I'll speak to Mr. and Mrs. Rogers at the gymkhana meeting tonight," she promised. "But I'm afraid it'll be too tiring to ride there and back in one day. If possible, would you like to make an overnight of it?" A cheer went up from all the girls.

That evening, on the way to the camp owners' cabin, Linda discussed the matter with Bob, Kathy, and Larry. They also were eager to make the trip with their campers, so Linda asked permission for the Old Sol group to lead the overnight trip.

"Don't go on the main road," Mr. Rogers advised them.

He produced a map of the area showing various trails and shortcuts in the vicinity of the ranch from where the lamb and goat had come. He traced a route with a pencil and handed the map to Linda.

"This will save you many miles," he said.

Mrs. Rogers added, "Since we're holding the gymkhana tomorrow afternoon, suppose you go the following day, when lunch and rest period are over."

"Thank you very much," said Linda. "I think it will be an exciting adventure."

For the next half hour, they made plans for the gymkhana. Because of it, there would be no riding instruction during the morning. Instead, the campers would be kept busy with swimming, dancing, tennis, and craft work.

Linda had been debating whether or not to report to the Rogerses how she and Bob had trailed Fred Newcombe and been hit by the yucca. She decided against it. Since there was no absolute proof to offer against the man, why worry them?

As soon as the counselors left the cabin, however, they talked over the matter among themselves and agreed with Linda to wait. The conversation now turned to how they would use their free time the next morning.

"I'd like to track down just where that ghost town is," said Linda, "and see if it has anything to do with the stagecoach stops. Anybody like to come along?

Larry spoke up at once. "I haven't done any sleuthing with you. I think it's my turn."

"And I have a suggestion to make to Miss Katherine Hamilton," said Bob with a grin. "Why don't we ride up the mountain to that spot where I saw Newcombe talking to Rink and see what we can find out?"

"I'd love it," said Kathy.

The next morning, Linda and Larry wasted

no time setting off in his car. When they reached Isabella, they made several inquiries about the two-horse stagecoach route that had run from that town to Onyx. No one knew where any of the stops had been.

Disappointed, the couple headed for Onyx. On the way, they saw a young man riding horseback along the side of the road. Larry pulled up and asked him about the stage stations.

The rider shook his head. "I've lived here all my life," he said, "but I'm not sure. I guess you'll have to find the old Indian who wanders all over this area. He seems to know everything, and if you can get him to talk, he may be able to give you some information."

"What's his name?" Linda asked.

"Mountain Dove." As the girl nodded knowingly, the man said, "You've heard of him?"

Linda smiled. "I've met him, but he preferred to talk to my friend and brother."

The horseman suggested that if Linda and Larry turned around and drove back slowly, they might see Mountain Dove. "As I came along, he was trudging through a meadow about a mile from here. He's a very bashful old fellow. If he sees anyone coming, he's apt to hide behind a tree."

Larry laughed. "That would account for our not having seen him."

The car was backed around and the searchers drove off. Larry kept his speed down to twenty miles an hour so that Linda could look carefully for Mountain Dove. She had about given up hope of spotting him when suddenly she saw a figure dart behind a large cottonwood.

"Stop!" she exclaimed.

Larry pulled to the side of the road and parked. "You saw him?" he asked.

"Maybe—maybe not. That tree over there— someone ran behind it. Larry, would you mind going to look? If I go, Mountain Dove won't say a word, but you may be able to get something out of him."

With a grin, Larry set off across the meadow, heading straight for the cottonwood. Linda watched eagerly and was rewarded a few moments later by seeing Mountain Dove step from behind the tree. By Larry's gestures, she knew that he was trying to glean the wanted information from the old Indian.

Presently, Larry signaled Linda to come to them. She hurried over.

"Maybe you can understand Mountain Dove better than I can," Larry said.

Linda paid strict attention as the Indian spoke and finally was able to piece together the information he gave. He explained that several small spur roads had run from the main route of the stage line.

"All gone," the Indian said. "Nobody use now."

Larry asked the Indian if there had ever been any stage stops along the spurs.

Mountain Dove nodded. "Coach stop at town."

Suddenly, as if bored by the whole conversation, he turned and walked off across the meadow.

"Afraid I didn't get much out of him," said Larry.

"Oh, I think you did," Linda answered. Her voice took on a note of excitement. "There must be some trace left of those old roads and of the town he mentioned. It might be the ghost town! Oh, Larry, I can hardly wait to visit it!"

The couple returned to the car and Larry drove at a snail's pace so they could try to locate any evidence of the old side roads.

In about twenty minutes, Linda's keen eyes detected an overgrown, tree-shaded, tangled opening. "I'll bet this is one!" she exclaimed. "I'd love to follow it!"

Larry studied the opening. "It should lead in the direction of the ghost town, if that ranch woman was giving us a straight story," he said.

"But it would be impossible for us to drive in there, and we wouldn't have time to make it on foot." Reluctantly, Linda agreed and the two headed back toward Saddle Creek Camp.

In the meantime, Kathy and Bob had ridden up the mountain and reached the spot where he had seen the meeting between Fred Newcombe, Jr., and Rink and the passenger in the truck.

"There doesn't seem to be anybody around now," Kathy remarked. "Do you think it's safe for us to go on?"

"The trail certainly doesn't stop the way Fred said it did," Bob answered. "Let's try it!"

The two went ahead, with Bob leading the way on the narrow but well-defined path. On either side, trees grew sparsely among big boulders. Gradually, the open slopes gave way to a thick growth, rendering the trail barely visible. There were horseshoe prints, however, indicating that someone had ridden on the path recently.

Suddenly, they spotted a wire fence straight ahead. A printed sign was nailed to one of the wooden gate posts.

PRIVATE PROPERTY
NO TRESPASSING
DANGER!
BLASTING!

The two riders came to a halt, amazed not only at the sign but at the intense stillness.

"There isn't any sound of blasting," Bob remarked skeptically. "I think we *should* trespass if we expect to clear up this mystery." He started toward the gate.

"Wait!" Kathy begged. "We might get near the spot where they're setting off dynamite. Even if *we* weren't hurt, the explosion would probably frighten our horses."

"Guess it is too risky," Bob conceded. "But listen!"

Somewhere ahead, and seemingly below them, the two could hear the whinnying of a lone horse. At once, Kathy sat up straight in her saddle. "That's a cry of protest!" she said. "What do you suppose is going on?"

The riders sat still, looking across the gate in hopes of learning an answer to the question.

Suddenly, Kathy, who had pulled up alongside Bob, grabbed his arm. She whispered, "Look over there by those trees! I think that's Rink in his Tyrolean hat! He's leading two palomino colts—maybe the ones Linda saw!"

The man apparently had not spotted the two riders. At least, he did not come in their direction. Instead, he turned the other way and disappeared among the trees.

"Shall we follow him?" Bob asked.

"I hate to act like a scaredy-cat," Kathy said, "but we really don't know what we might be getting into." Then she added, "Where do you think Rink's taking those colts this time?"

Bob was of the opinion that these were not the same two animals Linda had seen in the van. "From what she told me, I believe these are much smaller and younger. Maybe that cry we heard was from a mare that's the dam of one of them."

"Perhaps there's a horse farm around here," Kathy said. "Only why would anyone be blasting near such a place?"

"It's a riddle we can't figure out today, I'm afraid," Bob replied. "I don't want you to be in any danger. We'll go back and return another time when there are more of us."

"Yes, there's safety in numbers," Kathy said with a sigh.

The couple rode into Saddle Creek Camp just as Linda and Larry arrived. After they had told one another their adventures, Linda suggested that possibly the older Newcombe's 3 C H Ranch might have meadowland on the mountain.

"And you think he put that 'No Trespassing' sign and fence up just to keep people away?" Bob guessed.

"Yes," Linda replied.

"But why would the Newcombes be so secretive?" Kathy asked. "I should think they'd be proud to show off such beautiful palomino colts."

"And how is Rink involved?" Linda mused. "Does he work at the ranch?"

"I'm convinced something shady is going on," said Larry. "We're getting nearer the truth all the time."

"But," Linda cautioned, "we'd better not let Fred, Jr., suspect it. He may take some dangerous action against us."

The four friends decided to keep an even closer watch on the man from now on. "He got away from Bob and me once!" said Linda, "but he won't do it again!"

During the luncheon hour, excitement ran high among the campers over the gymkhana competition to be held that afternoon. First there would be a parade in costume, with each tent trying to outdo the other. This would be followed by the games.

Since there was to be a prize for the tent having the most original costumes, the participants were secretive about what they would wear. Linda, Kathy, and Bob had told one another what outfits their boys and girls would have on. Linda's group, they were sure, would look demure in their long, pioneer women's dresses and big sunbonnets. Kathy's would be Indian maidens, while Bob's would represent "city slickers" of the old West.

Larry, however, refused to say what the boys in his tent would wear. Linda was as curious to know as her young campers, who reported Larry had been all over borrowing clothes, getting pots and pans from the kitchen, and even some gold paint from the craft shop.

"You *really* don't know what Larry's boys will wear?" Anna Marie asked Linda.

The young counselor shook her head and laughed. "I can't wait to see them." Then she became serious.

"Before we leave, I'd like to tell you what is expected in the gymkhana. There are two ways to play the games—fairly and courteously, or rudely, due to overeagerness. I don't have to say which way I expect from all of you."

Linda reminded the girls that they were responsible not only for their own actions, but for those of their horses as well.

"Don't lose your temper and show it by mistreating your mount. And above all, listen carefully to the rules and follow them."

A bugle sounded. There was a last-minute flurry as each girl checked her costume.

"Here we go!" Linda said. "Good luck!"

She and her pioneers hurried to a large

meadow at the north end of the camp. Here Mr. and Mrs. Rogers, Fred Newcombe, and all the counselors who were not participating sat in chairs at one side. They were to act as judges.

Linda and Kathy lined up the various groups. Some were on foot, some on horseback.

Finally, the parade was ready to start. A record player with a marching tune was turned on. To loud applause, each group passed the reviewing stand, then took a position at the end of the field.

Larry's boys came last. As they entered on horseback and paraded toward the reviewing stand, campers and judges burst into howls of laughter.

A Camper's Secret 13

The five boy riders from Larry's tent wore baggy trousers, many sizes too large for them, held around their waists by ropes.

"Where in the world did they ever get those?" asked Mrs. Rogers, laughing merrily.

Faded, colored shirts and large battered felt hats completed their outfits. The boys also wore wigs of shoulder-length hair, shaggy false eyebrows, handlebar mustaches, and chest-length beards.

"Look what they're carrying!" cried Anna Marie.

Strapped to the side of each horse was either a pick or a shovel, together with a frying pan or stew pot. The last boy in line held a half-open gunnysack. In it lay a pile of gold nuggets.

"Are they real?" Susan asked.

Linda, who was standing near her, laughed. "I believe they're actually gilded pebbles. That's why Larry borrowed gold paint from the craft shop."

The campers, some on foot, some on horseback, paraded several times in a big circle. Finally, they were told to halt. Mr. Rogers arose and held up his hand for attention.

"I want to congratulate you on your fine costumes," he said. "You each should have a prize, but we arranged to award only one for this part of our gymkhana. It goes to the tent we have chosen as putting on the best act. Will the boys in Art Smith and Larry Spencer's tent please come forward?"

There was wild applause as the five riders turned their horses and came forward to the reviewing stand. Mr. Rogers handed a large box of assorted cookies and candied fruits to Skipper McKinley.

"Thank you very much, sir," said Skipper, grinning. "This is swell. We'll have a feast!"

The children were given a few minutes to remove their costumes, which they had put on over their riding clothes. Then the gymkhana games began. Bob and Larry would direct those for the boys, while Linda and Kathy would take care of the girls. Linda happened to glance over at Fred Newcombe, and thought he looked somewhat disgruntled. A few moments later, she noticed the riding master hurriedly leaving the grounds.

Is he just disgusted or jealous or is he up to something? Linda asked herself.

Her attention was recalled to the gymkhana by an announcement from Bob. He announced that the first event would be a barrel race for the boys. Five would compete at a time.

As Larry was placing five small open-end barrels at the far end of the meadow, Bob told Larry's tent group to mount up.

"What you must do is race to the barrel directly opposite you, dismount, ground-tie your horse, and tell it to stand still until you've crawled through the barrel and remounted. Then race back here to the finish line."

The contestants were loudly cheered, with campers calling out the names of their favorites. One horse kicked its barrel so that it rolled some distance away, slowing down his rider. Another refused to stand still and started back across the meadow. The only racer to make a perfect score was Skipper McKinley.

All the other boys in camp had their turns, and in the final runoff Roscoe came out the winner and received a blue ribbon.

As the happy boy grinned broadly, Linda thought, I'm sure Roscoe will never act the part of a bully again.

Next came a boots-and-saddle race for the girls. Kathy's group would ride first, with five other girls holding their horses at the opposite side of the meadow. The saddles lay on the ground beside the animals.

At the starting line, Kathy's contestants waited with their boots standing alongside them. Instructions were given and a whistle blew.

Instantly, each girl reached down for one boot, yanked it on, then did the same with the mate. This done, she started running furiously across the meadow. Reaching her horse, each girl had to saddle up, being sure to tie the latigo correctly, mount, and gallop back to the starting line.

Again, there were many mishaps. One girl forgot to tie the latigo on her horse and she was tossed off but not hurt. Another camper went limping across the field with one boot half-on and was disqualified.

Linda announced that only one girl, Grace Lawrence, had carried out the instructions perfectly. After all the contestants had tried this race, three of them were asked to compete in the finals. Grace won the event and received the blue ribbon to loud applause.

"We have one more game," Bob announced. "Boys and girls both may enter. It's called 'Musical Tires.'"

While he was speaking, Larry and some of the boy campers rolled out several old automobile tires from a nearby storage shack and laid them down in a row across the meadow.

"This game will be played to music," Bob explained. "You will canter clockwise around the ring. When we shut off the record player, you must quickly dismount and jump inside the tire nearest you. Since there is one less tire than there are riders, one person will be left out each time."

Five boys and five girls took their places. Linda called out, "There's one particular rule. You must always go forward, never backward, to get to a tire, and never leave your horse."

A lively tune was turned on and played for about a minute before Kathy shut off the machine. Some of the boys and girls were fortunate enough to be next to tires. They dismounted and jumped into them, happy that they had not been left out.

Anna Marie and a girl named Judy ran frantically, dragging their horses, and trying to reach the one empty at the end. As Anna Marie neared it, her horse suddenly balked and she was unable to reach the goal and jump safely inside before her opponent did. She laughed and walked to the reviewing stand.

The game went on for some time. As the number of losers grew, they cheered those who were left. Finally, there was only one tire lying in the meadow. Roscoe and Davy were the remaining contenders. Kathy let the music play longer than usual. It stopped abruptly.

Davy was a little quicker than Roscoe. He jumped from his horse and into the ring a fraction of a second before Roscoe did. The applause was loud and long. All the campers and onlookers declared it had been a wonderful and exciting gymkhana.

After Mr. Rogers had awarded the last blue ribbon, he said, "Linda, I have a special request from the campers—that you put on a show of your own with your trick palomino."

Linda smiled. "All right. I'll get Chica."

"I'll do it," Larry offered. "Is the stable locked?"

"I suppose so," Linda answered. She took off the key for the padlock from her shirt pocket and handed it to Larry.

He hurried off and returned in a few minutes, riding the beautiful golden horse. The campers clapped, then became silent as Linda mounted and trotted the horse in circles to limber her up.

Then, after a signal to Kathy, a waltz tune began to play and Linda led her filly into a graceful dance. The palomino kept perfect time in a sidestepping movement, then in a swaying motion, and finally in lifting her forelegs in flawless rhythm. As the music ended, Chica d'Oro made a deep bow.

The campers went wild and Susan cried out, "Chica is just like a circus horse!"

"That was a marvelous exhibition," said Mrs. Rogers, as horse and rider came forward.

Linda dismounted, and she and her filly took a bow together. Then Chica raised her upper lip in a good horse laugh.

The children screeched in merriment and demanded, "More! More!"

At this, the palomino turned toward Linda, plucked her kerchief from her pocket and swung it up and down in the air as if waving a flag. The applause and laughter were thunderous.

"She's just the most wonderful horse in the whole world!" cried Anna Marie.

At this moment, Roscoe came up. "Linda," he said, "may I walk Chica around to cool her off, and stable her?"

Linda patted the boy on the shoulder. "That's very kind, Roscoe," she said. "I'll be happy to have you do it."

The boy's face shone as he led Chica away. In twos and threes the other campers followed with their mounts.

The Old Solers stopped to chat with the Rogerses, who praised them highly for the fine way in which they had conducted the gymkhana. Finally, the camp owners left to go to their cabin.

The young instructors then started toward the stables to check on their horses. They had gone only fifty feet when Anna Marie came running toward them. She was out of breath and tears were streaming down her face.

"What's the matter?" Linda asked.

"Chica d'Oro got away from Roscoe!" Anna Marie sobbed. "Your beautiful horse went galloping off in the woods!"

Linda's heart sank as she rushed toward the stables. Fred Newcombe was there, quizzing Roscoe.

Seeing Linda, the boy exclaimed, "I didn't mean to do it! I couldn't help it! Chica just all of a sudden pulled away from me and went off in those woods!" He pointed toward a heavy growth of trees.

Bob was grim-faced. "We must organize a search party at once," he said. "We'll have to go on foot, but we mustn't lose track of one another."

Fred Newcombe did not offer to go and forbade Bill Shane from accompanying the searchers. Bill, though obviously displeased, was obligated to comply. The two swimming counselors joined the Old Solers and the group spread out. For nearly an hour, they combed the woods, calling Chica d'Oro's name and whistling for her. There was no responding whinny from the palomino.

Linda and Bob finally signaled the others to come together and confer on what to do next.

The swimming counselors felt that they should not be away any longer and hurried back to camp.

After they had left, Linda asked, "Do you think Mr. Newcombe, Sr., could have carried out his threat to get Chica?"

"He might have," said Bob. "But he did say he'd let you keep her until your stay at camp was over."

"Just the same, I'm suspicious. I believe we should inform Mr. and Mrs. Rogers right away, then notify the authorities."

The foursome hurried to camp and went to the owners' cabin. Upon hearing of Newcombe, Sr.'s threat, the couple were horrified and agreed that the police should be told at once. Linda hurried to the phone. She requested the officer who took the call to stop every horse van or trailer on the roads, and told about the warning she had received from the ranch owner. "I'd also appreciate your going to the 3 C H and checking." The officer agreed to make an investigation.

As the Old Solers walked off, Kathy said to Linda, "There's nothing we can do now but wait. Try to take it easy, honey."

But Linda spent a worried evening and a sleepless night. Before breakfast the next morning, she hurried to the Rogerses' cabin to find out if any report had come to them regarding the whereabouts of her talented horse.

"I telephoned headquarters a few minutes ago," Mr. Rogers told her. "Unfortunately, there is no trace of Chica d'Oro."

Mrs. Rogers looked sympathetically at Linda. "I know how you feel, dear," she said. "And I wish we could do more to help you."

"Perhaps you can," the girl said quickly. "Would it be possible for you to switch the children's riding lessons to this afternoon and let Bob, Kathy, Larry, and me search for Chica this morning?"

"I can arrange that," Mr. Rogers spoke up. "I'll mention it to Fred Newcombe."

Linda was sure the riding master would not like the plan. But being very suspicious of him now, she did not care what he might say.

"Where are you going to search?" Mrs. Rogers asked her.

Linda told about Bob and Kathy's finding of the gate marked "Danger," the whinnying of a horse nearby, and of their having seen Rink up there with palomino colts. "I think the place is worth investigating," she said.

Mr. Rogers remarked that the trip might be hazardous. "I insist that you take a state trooper along. I'll phone at once and ask an officer to come here. He can meet you at the stables."

The camp owner told Linda to pick out any horse she wanted to ride and then wished the girl the best of luck in her quest.

"Thank you," said Linda and dashed off to tell Bob and the others of the planned search for Chica d'Oro. The trip to the ghost town was postponed.

Linda was almost too excited to eat breakfast and during the meal kept mulling over the mystery. Suddenly, a new idea came to her. As the campers filed out of the dining hall, she said to Bob, "I'd like to speak to Roscoe alone. Would you please have him come down to the bridge?"

"I'll be glad to," her brother said, and hurried off.

When Roscoe arrived, he looked worried. "I couldn't help it, Linda!" he said at once. "Honest!"

"I didn't bring you here to scold you," said Linda kindly. "Of course, you know how bad I feel, and I also realize that you would do everything possible to get Chica d'Oro back. Now perhaps you can help me."

A look of fright flitted across Roscoe's face. "You—you aren't going to ask me to go hunting alone in the woods?" he asked.

"Gracious, no. I only called you here to see if maybe you could give me some clue as to where Chica d'Oro might have gone." Linda looked intently at Roscoe. "Did somebody frighten my horse and make her run away?"

The boy hung his head and scraped the toe of his moccasin on the wooden floor of the bridge. Finally, he said shamefacedly, "Chica didn't run off by herself. I was just walking her near the woods, when a man with a sort of a little Swiss hat came rushing out. He grabbed the reins and told me if I squealed on him I'd get hurt. Then he mounted your horse and galloped away among the trees."

Linda was stunned. She thought, Rink again!

Another suspicion crossed her mind, and she asked Roscoe, "Did you think up the idea of walking Chica?"

Roscoe looked down in the ravine as he replied, "No, I didn't. Mr. Newcombe told me maybe you'd let me have the honor of doing it, and said just where I should walk Chica, which was near the woods."

Linda gave Roscoe a little hug which made him blush furiously. "Thanks a million, Roscoe!" she said and dashed off to the stables.

Standing in the doorway was Bill Shane. Linda rushed up and asked where the riding master was.

"He just left here," Shane replied. "Fred seemed to be in a mighty big hurry."

"Where did he go?"

"He didn't say. Acted like something special came up. He rode out of here like a swarm of bees was chasing him!"

A Rewarding Search   14

Linda felt that she knew why the riding master had left in such a hurry—Mr. Rogers must have told him where the Craigs and their friends planned to go.

Fred has gone to warn the horse thief! she thought.

Nevertheless, she continued to quiz the groom and learned that Fred had gone into the woods along the trail that she knew led up to the danger gate.

Chica must be up there! Linda told herself excitedly. Up where Kathy and Bob had heard another horse whinny!

At this moment, the two appeared with Larry. Linda told them what she had learned from Roscoe and Shane. They were amazed and incensed.

Bob said, "We must go after that double-crosser as fast as possible! He has too much of a head start already. Let's go! Now!"

The four young people hurried into the stables and saddled their horses to be ready to leave the instant the trooper arrived.

The searchers were irked by the delay, but in a few minutes two officers drove in. They parked and walked over to the stables.

The men introduced themselves as Donahoe and West. They asked to be briefed on the exact nature of the search. Bob told them the full story and Linda added her suspicions about the riding master.

"He took the very trail we want to follow. Maybe we can catch up to him before he has a chance to notify any confederates."

"Let me get this straight, Miss Craig," said Trooper West. "You mean you think Fred Newcombe, Jr., is responsible for the theft of your palomino?"

"Yes. And we suspect he may be up to some other underhanded work."

Officer Donahoe frowned. "Then let's get started. I understand that we can borrow two of the camp's horses."

Bob took the men inside and helped them select two bays. As soon as they were saddled, the six riders started off. They reached the danger gate without seeing Newcombe or anyone else.

Trooper West frowned, puzzled. "I don't understand this sign," he said. "As far as I know, no person in this area has a license to set off explosives."

The gate was opened and the search continued. A short distance farther on, the crude trail branched.

Kathy said excitedly, "This is the place where Bob and I saw Rink leading two palomino colts!"

"That's right," said Bob.

Everyone dismounted and hunted for fresh horseshoe prints. They found several along the upper trail and a number also on the branch.

"What are we going to do now?" Larry asked.

Trooper West suggested that they divide forces. He would accompany Linda and Bob on the upper trail while Donahoe would lead Kathy and Larry downward along the branch.

The two groups started off. After a short ride, the Craigs and the officer with them came to a break among the tall firs through which they had been riding. Below them stretched a green, fenced-in meadow. Grazing in it were several sorrel, bay, and Arabian mares, some palomino colts, and a beautiful palomino stallion. Disappointed, Linda saw that Chica d'Oro was not among them. Then, suddenly, the girl caught her breath as she noticed the stallion shake his head from side to side while nibbling the grass.

She grabbed Bob's arm. "Isn't that King, the

valuable horse that has been missing for a year?" she asked.

Instantly, not only her brother but the trooper was extremely interested. They stared down into the meadow and watched the horse.

Finally, Officer West said grimly, "This animal exactly fits the description and pictures of King in our files. That peculiarity he has while eating makes him pretty identifiable."

"We must rescue King at once!" said Linda. "Probably all those mares were stolen, too!"

Trooper West held up his hand. "I'll have to ask you and your brother to stay a safe distance behind me while I go to investigate."

The trail led down the slope, then alongside the high barbed wire fence to a crude barn. Going through the building was the only way into the meadow, for the wire barrier extended unbroken to the sides of the barn.

Obeying orders, the Craigs rode some distance behind the trooper. Just as they reached the bottom of the slope, Rink came out of the barn. He was astride a black horse and was leading a string of palomino colts. Before the man knew what was happening, the officer spurred ahead, seized the bridle of his mount, and told Rink he was under arrest.

"Arrest!" Rink whined. "What for? I haven't done anything to break the law!"

"We'll see about that," the trooper replied

shortly. "We know you have the stolen horse, King."

When Rink heard this, he went pale. Suddenly, he let out a bellow which made all the horses jump.

Linda and Bob exchanged glances. Was Rink signaling to someone in the barn? Just then, Linda saw a man dash out from the rear door into the meadow and race across it.

"That's Rink's pal—the one we saw with the palomino colts in Weldon!" she exclaimed. "Come on, Bob, let's stop him!"

The Craigs dismounted, and ground-hitched the horses. They helped each other climb between two strands of barbed wire and raced across the meadow after the fleeing man. Although they were gradually gaining on him, the fugitive was still some three hundred yards ahead. Suddenly, they heard a shout behind them, and looked back to see if reinforcements had come for Rink and his pal. There was no one in sight. Again the Craigs thought that Rink might have been warning a confederate, but saw no one. As they turned back to continue their pursuit, the two stopped short in amazement.

Their quarry had disappeared!

"Where could he have gone?" Linda asked. "There are no trees or boulders or bushes in this meadow. It's perfectly flat."

Her brother was as puzzled as she. The fence at the opposite end of the meadow was some distance ahead of where they had last seen the fleeing man.

Suddenly, a thought came to Linda. "Bob," she said, "have you ever heard of a cutback creek?"

"You mean those deep gullies in the middle of a meadow—the ones that are dry most of the time?"

"Yes."

At once Bob caught her idea. "You think the man we were chasing might have dropped into one?"

"That's my guess. Let's hurry and find out!"

The two went forward on a run. As Linda had guessed, there was a dry creek about five feet deep and overgrown with grass. Crouched in it was the runaway!

The instant the stranger realized he had been spotted, he started to climb the far embankment. Bob made a flying leap for him and caught the man before he reached the top.

"What do you want with me?" he snarled, as Linda rushed up.

"Why were you running away from us?" Bob asked him.

"I ain't done nothing. You got no right to hold onto me. Get your hands off!"

Bob released his grip as Linda said, "Suppose you tell us what you're doing here. We know you're part of a group that stole the stallion, King, and my palomino, Chica d'Oro."

The man looked frightened. "I had to do these things—they made me."

"By *they* you mean Fred Newcombe and Rink?" Bob asked him.

"Yes, yes. They threatened to—to kill me if I didn't do what they told me to!"

Linda remarked, "When we saw you and Rink with the colts in Weldon, you seemed to be the boss. Were both you and Rink taking orders from Fred Newcombe?"

The man refused to answer this question, and would not give his name. Suddenly, he lashed out at Bob with a hard punch intended for the youth's chin. Instinctively, Bob dodged, but came back with a strong uppercut which sent the fellow flying.

With a look of hate, he picked himself up. "All right, you win the first round," he muttered. "I'll go with you."

The prisoner was made to march in front of Linda and Bob to the barn. They prodded him through the building and came out where Trooper West and Rink were waiting with the palomino colts.

"Good work!" said the officer to the Craigs. "Did you get a confession?"

Bob smiled. "Yes."

Hearing this, Rink turned malevolently on the other prisoner. "Why, you low-down double-crosser! Why'd you talk—these folks didn't have a thing on us till you squealed!"

His pal refused to answer.

"Where's Newcombe?" the trooper asked sharply. But neither man would reply.

"I'll search the barn," Bob volunteered, "to be sure none of the gang is hiding there." He hurried inside, but soon returned. "No luck," he said.

After Linda and Bob had returned the palomino colts to the meadow, the prisoners were tied back to back.

"Walk!" Trooper West ordered as he swung into his saddle. "You can turn around every ten minutes so neither of you will have to walk backward for long."

The Craigs went to their horses, mounted, then followed the officer and his prisoners.

When they reached the branching trail, Linda said to the trooper, "If you can manage these men alone, would it be all right for Bob and me to go down this path and find out what happened to our friends and Officer Donahoe?"

"Go ahead." West grinned. "When I think that once I worried whether or not you could take care of yourselves, it makes me smile!"

With the prisoners giving them baleful looks, the Craigs galloped off. Fifteen minutes later, they overtook the trio resting beside a small stream.

"Did you see anyone?" Linda called out. "Or get a clue to Chica?"

Kathy showed her disappointment. "No, but we're still following horseshoe prints. Did you have any luck?"

When she and Larry and Trooper Donahoe heard about the capture, they exclaimed in amazement.

"And both confessed," Linda added. "Our suspicions about Fred Newcombe were correct all along. He was running this little racket up in the mountains. *That's* why he wanted his friends to come to Saddle Creek Camp as riding instructors, so nobody would go snooping around, as we did. I presume he made things so unpleasant for the former group of instructors that they left."

"You mean," said Larry, "that Rink and his pal admitted having stolen Chica?"

Linda's eyes clouded with worry. "Yes. But they wouldn't talk about it. She wasn't up in the meadow. I have a good hunch she was there and Newcombe took her away to keep us from finding her. Maybe that's what he did when he left camp in such a hurry."

"Where could he have taken her?" Larry wondered.

"Down this trail?" Kathy asked.

Trooper Donahoe pointed out the horseshoe prints ahead of them. There were two sets, one heavy, the other light.

"I'd say that only the first horse was being ridden," he remarked. "The one behind was on a lead line."

Linda examined the prints. The second set was small. "Chica!" she exclaimed.

Linda was so excited to think they were on the trail of her beautiful filly that she was eager to set off at once.

"All right," Officer Donahoe agreed. "But if we're getting close to where she's being held, Newcombe or whoever has your horse may put up a fight. You girls ride at the rear."

As the procession set off, Kathy went ahead of Linda but turned halfway in the saddle to ask, "Did you find out from those prisoners where this trail leads?"

"No," Linda replied, "but I have a strong hunch that it will bring us right to the 3 C H Ranch."

Her chum gasped. "That means we're riding right into big trouble! Mr. Newcombe, Sr., must be in on the plot, too!"

The girls became silent. Tension mounted during the long ride through the woods. Suddenly, the trees gave way to open meadows with ranch buildings in the distance. The trooper, in the lead, put his horse into a gallop.

The others took his cue and hurried out into the sunlit meadow.

Linda, last in line, was the only one who noticed a small stable nestled among the trees a little distance from the trail. It occurred to her that this might be the place where the palomino colts from the meadow were kept until they were taken away to be sold.

Chica d'Oro might be hidden in there! she told herself.

Linda had slowed down, and turned back toward the stable. The other riders did not notice that she was no longer following them. When she reached the little building, Linda dismounted and entered the dim interior. For a moment, after the bright daylight, she could see nothing. Then she blinked in amazement and joy.

"Chica!" Linda cried out, and rushed toward the filly, who was in a crude stall.

The horse gave a whinny in greeting, but before Linda could reach her, a figure stepped out of the shadows and stood beside the palomino. Fred Newcombe! One arm was raised and in his hand he carried a wicked-looking club. The riding master's jaw was set and his eyes glittered menacingly.

"Linda Craig," he said, "if you come one step nearer, I'll lame your horse so she'll never walk again!"

Ghost Town Treasure 15

For a few moments, Linda was paralyzed with terror at Newcombe's threat to Chica d'Oro. The thought of her filly's being crippled was more than she could bear. Her brain raced desperately for a way out of the dilemma. Finally, she decided on a bargaining tactic.

"You plan to sell Chica d'Oro, don't you?" Linda said. "How can you if you harm her?"

The riding master had not expected this retort, and stared into space as he sought an answer. Linda seized the opportunity of inching forward.

"You can get a tremendous sum of money for her, you know," Linda went on, moving closer to the stall.

She now noticed that the horse was not tied. Fred held Chica's halter in his free hand. As Linda watched the man closely, she could see his fingers relaxing. Now was her chance!

Linda cried out, "Chica! Run! Run!"

Instantly, the filly yanked away from the man and raced from the stable. Linda did not wait to see Fred's reaction, but ran out, leaped onto her borrowed horse, and raced after Chica. She caught up, grabbed the filly's halter, and kept going at a full gallop.

"You'll be sorry for this!" Fred shouted. "I'll get even with you if it's the last thing I do!"

Linda did not even turn her head. She wanted to put as much distance between her and the man as possible. Across the meadow she could see her group. Suddenly, Kathy turned, saw Chica d'Oro, and called to the others. They wheeled and galloped to meet her.

"You found Chica!" Kathy cried. "Where? How did you do it?"

Linda quickly told her story, and everyone rode back to the stable. But Newcombe had disappeared.

"There isn't any place he could hide but the woods," said Linda. "He must have gone up the trail."

"I'll go after him!" said Trooper Donahoe. "Bob, Larry, want to come along?"

"You bet," both boys answered.

"Wait here for us," Bob directed the girls.

They were happy to do so. Linda ground-hitched her borrowed horse, then went to stroke Chica.

"Baby, you've had a dreadful experience,"

she said. "I thought we were guarding you so well, but those awful men got the better of us for a while."

Just then, she and Kathy became aware of a man riding across the meadow toward them from the ranch buildings. As he came closer, Linda said, "It's Fred Newcombe, Sr."

As he rode up, the ranch owner stared at Chica d'Oro. For an instant, the girls thought he looked startled and fearful. The next moment he recovered himself and said, "So you've come to your senses at last, Linda Craig? How much do you want for your filly?"

Linda looked the man straight in the eyes. "Your pretense won't do you any good, Mr. Newcombe. Your son and his friends stole my horse. Rink and the other men are on their way to jail. They've made a full confession."

The ranch owner swayed in the saddle. For a second, the girls thought he was going to fall off. Then his bravado returned. "Nonsense!" he said. "You don't expect me to believe that!"

"You'll find out very soon that I'm telling the truth," said Linda. "Besides, we believe *you* are involved. You used the mountain meadow to keep those fine mares and the stallion, King. Their palomino colts were brought down here, taken out and sold."

Mr. Newcombe was so angry that Kathy was sure he was going to strike Linda, and whispered, "We'd better get out of here!"

Linda was almost ready to take her friend's advice when Trooper Donahoe emerged from the woods with Fred Newcombe, Jr., handcuffed. His father groaned and buried his head against the horse's neck.

The riding master's jaw was set. Instead of showing any pity for his father, he cried out harshly, "I told you the idea wouldn't work! We might have got away with it if you hadn't been so greedy to get Chica d'Oro!"

The battle of words between father and son that followed provided a full confession of the dishonest operation they had carried on. It was learned that the truck driver, Mike Olson, was involved in the horse stealing, and worked part-time on the Newcombe ranch. His passenger, too, was part of the ring and helped sell the palomino colts. Rink and his pal were the two men Roscoe had overheard outside Larry's tent.

Further questioning revealed that Rink's companion had been the man Linda saw sneaking from the stables on the night of the poisoning. Both Newcombes admitted that if Linda, Bob, Kathy and Larry had not arrived at camp, they would have had their own friends instructing the children.

"It's lucky for the campers they didn't," said Linda, "and also that Mr. and Mrs. Rogers know my grandparents, so we could be asked to come here part of the season." She turned to Fred, Jr. "Was it you who put something in Rocket's drinking water to give him colic, and wiped acid on our horses' lips?"

The riding master, completely crestfallen, nodded. "And it wasn't Chica that kicked me. It was one of the camp horses."

Fred Newcombe, Sr., put up no resistance when handcuffs were fastened to his wrists. Officer Donahoe said he could handle the two prisoners and would not need any assistance. "We'll see that Olson and his pal are rounded up."

Bob asked, "What's going to happen to all those thoroughbred mares in the meadow? How about the four of us going up there and taking them to camp? Then the owners can come and claim them."

The trooper thought this over. "It's an excellent idea," he said. "Go ahead."

Donahoe mounted up and led off his captives, while Linda's group rode to the meadow. There, the foursome made pack trains of the mares, the colts, and Linda's borrowed horse.

Chica d'Oro's saddle was found hidden in a dark corner of the barn. Linda put it on the filly.

Bob smiled at his sister. "I think you've done more to solve this mystery than any of us. You should have the honor of bringing in King."

Linda laughed. "I accept!" she said and sprang into the saddle.

Leading the handsome stallion, she and Chica headed the procession along the trail which led to Saddle Creek Camp. When they neared the stables, the first person they met was Bill Shane, the groom. He stared in complete bewilderment.

"You found Chica d'Oro! And all these other horses . . . what—"

The man's amazement turned to incredulity when he learned that the camp's riding master had been taken to jail, and the reason for it.

"I never did like Fred," Shane said, "but I didn't suspect he was a crook! And I know Mr. and Mrs. Rogers didn't."

Two boy campers who had been outside the stables had seen the excitement. They raced from one tent to another to spread the news. Within ten minutes, every camper and counselor had gathered in the stable courtyard. The camp owners had been summoned by Larry.

"I just can't believe it!" exclaimed Mrs. Rogers after hearing a firsthand account of the arrest.

Her husband shook hands fervently with the Craigs and their friends and said, "I owe you a great debt of gratitude. It is regrettable that my counselors and campers had to put up with such a riding master. I'm afraid his smooth talk and plausible explanations had my wife and me fooled as to his real character."

Kathy, relieved and happy, said, "You didn't know it, but wherever Linda Craig and Chica d'Oro go, there's bound to be mystery and excitement."

Linda blushed and said quickly, "Don't you think we'd better take care of our horses? They've had a long, hard ride."

"Right, Sis." Bob grinned.

"How about yourselves?" Mrs. Rogers exclaimed. "It's mid-afternoon and you've had no lunch!" She hurried away to arrange a snack for them.

One by one the campers left, but Anna Marie stayed behind. She came over to Linda and squeezed her hand.

"You're just the most wonderful person in the world," she said. Then, looking earnestly into her counselor's eyes, she asked, "Will what happened keep us from our overnight?"

"No indeed," Linda replied, laughing softly. "Remember, we hope to find the lost treasure of gold at the ghost town!"

That evening, the trail maps were consulted again, and Linda was able to sketch in the weed-grown spur that probably had led from the main road to what was now the ghost town. To reach it, the riders would have to go to Kernville, cross the river, and take various trails along the northern shore of Lake Isabella.

"The trouble is," said Bob, who was poring over the map with his sister, "that there's no trail leading directly to the ghost town. It looks as if we'll have to blaze our own trail through the woods."

"In that case," said Larry, who had been listening, "we'd better take plenty of tools."

Kathy giggled. "Of course we will. How do you expect to dig up a treasure without any tools?"

The ghost-town trip would include all the campers in the Old Solers' tent. It was all they talked about the following day, which was Sunday.

Early Monday morning, two days' rations were packed in saddlebags and each person carried a bedroll. It was a crisp, clear morning, and everyone at Saddle Creek Camp was out to wave good-bye and wish the overnighters luck.

The arduous journey required many rest periods, and directly after lunch an hour was taken for a short nap. Refreshed, the riders pushed on through dense groves of trees, open country, and stony territory.

Late in the afternoon, the horses were once more proceeding through a thickly wooded area.

"You were right," Larry called to Bob in the rear. "There sure isn't any trail!"

"When *are* we going to get to the ghost town?" Roscoe asked impatiently.

"If our guess is correct," said Linda, "it should be at the other side of these woods."

The thought spurred the weary travelers on.

The positions in the line of riders had been changed several times, but by later afternoon Linda was in the lead with Susan and Skipper. By now, the woods were growing dark and seemed to stretch on endlessly.

I hope we haven't missed the ghost town, Linda thought.

A moment later, she caught sight of what she felt sure was the top of a weatherbeaten building.

"I think we've found it!" she shouted back excitedly.

Linda proceeded as quickly as she dared. Suddenly, before her eyes, in a weedy, overgrown clearing, were the ramshackle buildings of a ghost town! The most prominent one bore the faded sign, HOTEL. Its porch roof had caved in. Alongside it stood a store in a worse state of disrepair. Other buildings nearby were half-gone, with rubble lying about. Stairways were exposed, and many rooms were mere shells, with a scattered growth of wild flowers and ferns growing in them.

Soon all the counselors and campers had assembled in front of the ruins and stood gazing in awe. This did not last long. Several of the boys dismounted and made a beeline for the hotel, declaring that they wanted to see what was inside.

"Be careful!" Bob warned, and dashed after them. "Don't go on the stairway—it might collapse! And watch the floor for rotted boards!"

In a short time, all the campers were investigating the abandoned village. Suddenly, a shout was heard from inside the hotel.

"Look what I found!" Davy yelled as he rushed from the old structure, holding a large, musty-looking ledger. Everyone crowded around him. He laid the old record book on the ground and opened the cover.

"It's the hotel register!" Bob exclaimed.

He and Linda fell to their knees and began to examine the pages. They were stained from having been water-soaked, so many names were obliterated. Nevertheless, Linda turned sheet after sheet, running a finger down the entries that were still legible.

"They must have had lots of visitors," Susan remarked.

Suddenly, Linda gave a shout of triumph. "Here it is! The signature of Abner Stowe!"

A cheer went up from everyone, and Roscoe said excitedly, "We've found the right place! The sack of gold must be buried here!"

The children grabbed the various tools which

they had brought and began to dig here and there in the hard soil. There was complete silence as they worked feverishly. Bob, Larry, and Kathy watched, advising them now and then, looking as eagerly into the excavations as the campers did.

All this time, Linda had stood a short distance away. Her mind was trying to reconstruct the event that had happened at this spot so many, many years before. The stagecoach had drawn up in front of the hotel. Apparently, Abner Stowe was one of the first to alight, probably carrying a carpetbag and his sack of nuggets. He had hurried inside and registered. Then, hearing the noise of the robbers attacking the stagecoach, he had hastened somewhere to hide this treasure before the holdup men could raid the hotel.

But where would Abner have gone? she asked herself. Surely not out front. He may have ducked out the back door.

Linda darted between the hotel and the store and went a short distance in the rear of the two buildings. Here the ground was not so hard. Evidently, a stream had once run through, and even now the soil was marshy.

Old Abner could have buried his gold along the stream, where the digging would have been easier and quicker, Linda told herself.

She turned back quickly, located Bob, and

told him her idea. He brought spades, and the two began to dig. One by one, Kathy, Larry and the campers came to watch. They themselves had had no luck and were weary from turning up the hard-packed earth.

Hole after hole was made with no results. Bob said, "If we only had a good solid clue!"

No one could offer any suggestions, so the digging went on. Larry remarked that they should have brought a Geiger counter to locate the metal.

"But we didn't," said Linda. "I do have a hunch, though. See that big cottonwood over there? People who buried things often used trees as landmarks. Let's try that spot."

The digging operations were transferred to the base of the old tree. With renewed vigor, Linda set her spade into the ground, put her foot on the tool, and thrust it deep. Working quickly, she brought up several spadefuls of earth. Suddenly, the tool hit some obstruction.

Linda got down and brushed the dirt away. "Here's a metal box!" she exclaimed, hardly daring to believe her search had come to an end.

Bob and Larry helped her clear the area and lifted out the large box. On the top, barely visible, was the word HOTEL. One of the inn's small strongboxes! It was rusted and the lock had corroded. Everyone crowded around the box and watched breathlessly as Bob pried off the lid.

Linda and the others gasped. Inside lay a leather sack tied at one end with deer thong. Quickly, Linda unwound this and opened the bag as the children crowded closer.

"Gold nuggets!" Roscoe shouted, and started jumping up and down.

"Here's a note," said Linda, reaching one hand inside the sack and pulling out the paper. She was almost hoarse with excitement, but managed to read: "PROPERTY OF ABNER STOWE."

A tumult of shouts followed Linda's announcement. The boys threw their hats into the air with cries of "Yippie!" which could be heard across the valley. The girls hugged one another and danced around. Linda, Bob, Kathy, and Larry joined in the gaiety.

"How I wish Cactus Mac were here!" Linda said. "Can't you just see the big grin on his face when he hears the news!"

As Bob did a little jig, Anna Marie skipped over to the counselors. Her face was radiant. "This has been the best vacation ever!" she declared, and planted a kiss on Linda's suntanned cheek.

This seemed to be a signal for all the young campers to circle around the Rancho del Sol riders. They burst into camp songs, their faces flushed and happy. The spontaneous serenade ended with a mighty "R-R-R-RAH!"

THE LINDA CRAIG™ SERIES
by Ann Sheldon

You will also enjoy
NANCY DREW MYSTERY STORIES®
by Carolyn Keene